PRIMITIVE WAR DISPATCHES

THE HUNTING OF STALKER FORCE

-A short story anthology by Ethan Pettus-

-In memory of Rod Serling-

-Author's Note-

    The Hunting of Stalker Force is the first volume of Primitive War Dispatches, a series of serialized short-story anthologies meant to link the novels of the Primitive War series. Primitive War Dispatches Vol. 1 - The Hunting of Stalker Force takes place between Primitive War I and Primitive War II - Animus Infernal.

PROLOGUE – NIHIL RIVER GOD

1968, Vietnam.

The mangal forest was silent.

Andrei Wynn could scarcely believe what he was hearing. The mangroves were immobile, their branches rigid and stained dark from the prior night's rainfall. The interwoven canopies of the mangroves, leaves glimmering like soot-stained emeralds, hung like a listless cloud only ten feet over Andrei's head. The monkeys and birds that had provided a chorus for Andrei's journey had suddenly been transposed into shadowy gargoyles, paralyzed and mute within their arboreal roosts. Andrei momentarily paused amongst the mist-veiled trunks of the mangroves, looking across the silhouetted forms of driftwood logs.

Even the insects had lost their voice.

Andrei shook his head aggressively; he had greater things to fear than silence; and his hollow, rumbling gut begged him to press on. It had been three months since Andrei's superiors in the USSR had left him for dead within the valley, and the last of his rations had run out weeks ago. He had been frequenting the mangal forest in favor of the forested foothills of the valley, for there was scarce undergrowth to obscure visibility and there were plentiful crustaceans to be found among the skeletal roots of the mangroves. Andrei was beginning to second-guess his judgment, but he had already ventured too far from his research station. He refused to return empty-handed again.

Three months of sporadic dysentery, incremental starvation, and continual abuse of the research station's morphine supplies had quickly shaved off nearly thirty pounds from Andrei's emaciated frame. His USSR researcher's uniform was tattered and thread-bare, stained with piss from the waist-down and hanging from his body like afghan robes. Dark stripes and speckles of dried blood framed every laceration through Andrei's clothing; reminders of his near-brushes with the valley's ravenous predatory fauna.

Andrei lurched through the mist, pendulous arms swinging, a Makarov pistol clutched tightly in his right hand. A torrential thunderstorm had showered the valley over the past week, and the ground of the mangal forest was well-soused. The wet sand was a pleasant cushion beneath Andrei's worn-out soles, and the prospect of fresh food warmed his core.

He only wished he could shake the pervading menace of the silence.

Andrei could only force his legs to move at the pace of a brisk, limping walk. During his second month alone in the valley, a hormone-crazed stygimoloch had charged him full-speed and nearly broke his leg with its thorny skull. The fat-starved flesh of Andrei's pallid thigh still displayed a plum-hued, concave bruise. Andrei had injected some morphine before his journey to help quell the pain in his leg, but it did little to calm the cyclone swirling through his bowels.

Andrei dimly wondered how much morphine it would take to lose his fear.

Andrei dropped to his knees at the base of a mangrove tree and stuck his arms into the exposed root-ball. His slender fingers skimmed the muddy floor within, spider-legging around in search of a crab or a turtle he could crack open and eat raw. The silence of the forest amplified his rasping hyper-ventilations. Despite the morphine rendering his remaining musculature to putty, the excessive dopamine muddying his consciousness to sludge, the fear the silence had wrought continued to permeate throughout his core.

[2]

Crack.

Andrei flinched at the sound of a branch breaking under-foot. A voluminous growl sifted through the hazy clearing and tunneled through the intoxicated molasses of Andrei's mind. He could feel the subtle trembling of the approaching animal's footsteps running through the earth and up his extremities. The creature's horse-like huffing was interspersed by low, reptilian hissing.

Andrei looked in every direction but he only saw the endless mangroves standing crooked, black, and emaciated amongst the shriveled driftwood logs. The ringing tinnitus that followed the mysterious vocalization scared Andrei more than the sound itself had. He could hear the footsteps more clearly as they drew near, the clawed feet padding and scraping through the sand.

Running was as good as suicide; hiding was Andrei's only other option.

Andrei started squeezing his body into the mangrove tree's root ball, shimmying through the slick, constricting tendrils of bark to the dank center. His hyper-ventilations turned rabid, uncontrollable in volume or frequency. The adrenaline momentarily overpowered the morphine in Andrei's veins and gave way to a fresh flow of cold, paralyzing fear.

Fear was the base element of Andrei's existence.

Fear of starvation; fear of the dinosaurs he had brought into the world; fear of the Soviet military leaders he had served for the sake of a nihilist's Cold War. Andrei had been commissioned to build a particle-accelerator in war-torn Vietnam, and it had led him to ruin. Dinosaurs had been brought into their world through a catastrophic mistake; one that rested solely on Andrei's shoulders. Andrei's horrific guilt had been his only stead-fast comrade during his entire hellish banishment.

[3]

The only thing more horrific Andrei could imagine was being eaten alive.

Andrei huddled within the damp hollow of the mangrove and drew his Makarov pistol. He placed the barrel against his temple as he waited for the approaching dinosaur to materialize through the fog. Andrei understood more about the dinosaurs than any of the Russians in the valley did; he knew that he possessed zero chances of surviving an attack. The Makarov pistol was only good for ending his own life in the event of a mauling.

Suicide was preferable to the maulings that Andrei had witnessed.

Andrei's eyes darted across every surface visible beyond the mangrove. There were the stilted bodies of the other mangrove trees, the tangled roots like masses of fossilized serpents, ferns and palms sprouting from the sand around driftwood debris. An apparition began to manifest within the depths of the fog. The footsteps increased in volume, each footfall connecting with a thump of Andrei's tired heart. His eyes protruded dangerously from their sockets.

The apparition finally materialized through the mist, sauntering into the clearing with the eased gait attributable to apex predators. Andrei recognized the creature as a Kaprosuchus, an ancient crocodyliform with elongated limbs for terrestrial hunting and a blunted snout filled with tusk-like fangs. The kaprosuchus was a full-grown male, a solitary 'rogue' that frequented the waterways of the valley. The rogue's square jaws were heavily laden with shallow scars from constantly fighting other kaprosuchus for the lion's share in violent feeding-frenzies.

Andrei shivered as he watched the kaprosuchus pace around the clearing. The crocodilian predator's shoulders lolled easily beneath its armor-plated musculature. The pale-blue scutes and scales glinted dully as they captured what

[4]

little light fell through the low canopy. The rogue was as long as the BRDM-2 recon vehicles Andrei once rode in while serving the Soviets within the valley.

Andrei almost missed them.

The barrel of the Makarov was pinned against Andrei's temple. He watched as the kaprosuchus paced closer, the carnivore huffing and snorting with its snout held low to the ground like a pig in search of truffles. The kaprosuchus's snout traced Andrei's footprints through the soil, around the rotting carcasses of driftwood, closer to Andrei's make-shift shelter. Andrei inched back on his ass, the pistol teetering in his limpid grip.

Andrei froze.

The foliage behind the mangrove began to shift. Andrei didn't dare to look; the kaprosuchus had raised its head from the soil. The kaprosuchus was staring directly at him. The crocodilian beast opened its jaws and rumbled lowly from its cavernous chest. The kaprosuchus snapped its tusks through the mangrove's roots, tearing away a volley-ball sized chunk with a single bite.

Andrei cried out as the root-ball crackled and contorted around him. The kaprosuchus raked its claws through the soil, burrowing growling and snapping through the roots to Andrei's throat. Andrei scuttled back, the three-foot high ceiling providing no quicker form of mobility. The kaprosuchus rammed its head forward, growling with effort as it struggled to crawl through the constricting lattice to its morphine-soaked meal.

Andrei twisted around and started clambering out through the root ball, grasping for the soil beyond the wooden legs. He could feel the kaprosuchus's breath gusting up his backside, further dampening his shivering body. He could see the

[5]

ferns growing along the outer rim of the mangrove, just a few feet from his grasping fingers. If he could just get out of the root ball, he could try to climb a tree or make a run for it.

If Andrei couldn't run, he would take his own life.

Andrei felt the kaprosuchus's forefingers spread across his shoulder, and then the ripping pain of claws stripping through the flesh of his back. Andrei screamed as the shallow lacerations evaporated the numb of his high. He smacked his hands around the outer-most roots of the mangrove and dragged himself forward, hissing through his teeth as the kaprosuchus's claws tore free from the small of his back. He could see the fronds of the ferns only inches away, beyond the skeletal black roots…growing ever blacker…

The mass of ferns began to rise.

Andrei stared dimly as the vegetation unraveled before his eyes. The low-rumbling and guttural roars of the kaprosuchus fell deaf on his ears. Every sensation other than sight was washed from Andrei's mind as the foliage suddenly shifted into the shape of a towering dromaeosaurid.

Andrei had never known that utahraptors were in the valley.

The utahraptor circled the root-ball, its long wing-like arms hanging low and ready. Andrei's eyes scaled over the utahraptor's three-inch claws that adorned its grasping forefingers, the near-perfect feathers blanketing its bird-like frame. The utahraptor's reptilian jaws spread open as its glowing amber eyes locked onto Andrei.

The kaprosuchus was still snarling, snapping, panting and clawing through the root-ball, but all else was mute. The utahraptor carried the silence around its body like a second set of camouflage. Nothing dared to distract the dromaeosaurid on the hunt.

Andrei heard the kaprosuchus roar, and he dove away from the utahraptor.

The kaprosuchus burst forth from the root-ball in a shower of shattered bark and tackled into the utahraptor. The two titans rolled across the sandy clearing, the utahraptor's feathers flurrying loose from its body, grit spraying from their impact against the sand. Andrei couldn't think, couldn't move; the alchemy of morphine and shock transformed his limbs to lead. All he could do was sit and stare, the Makarov forgotten on the ground beside him as he listened to the carnivores bellow and howl.

The kaprosuchus climbed on top of the utahraptor, pinning it to the ground with its powerful forelimbs. The kaprosuchus snapped its jaws around the side of the utahraptor's head, penetrating the featherless skin around its skull. A scream erupted from beneath the kaprosuchus, and a well-placed swing from the utahraptor's forearm flayed some of the flesh from the kaprosuchus's snout.

The kaprosuchus let go of the utahraptor and reared its head back from the utahraptor's slashing forearms. The kaprosuchus slammed the palms of its fore-feet against the side of the utahraptor's neck, raking deep wounds through the dromaeosaurid's feathered mane with its claws. Glistening burgundy bubbled forth from the raw, exposed musculature tissue as the utahraptor screeched in deafening decibels.

The utahraptor kicked the kaprosuchus's abdomen, splitting open the soft underbelly with its six-inch toe claws. The gash spread open and coils of translucent pink intestine spilled onto the writhing utahraptor. The kaprosuchus arched back on its hind-legs, standing so high that its snout brushed the underside of the mangrove

[7]

canopy. The crocodilian howled in pain with enough force to make Andrei's spectacles tremble.

The kaprosuchus fell forward and slammed its jaws over the utahraptor's head. The kaprosuchus's tusks penetrated the utahraptor's scalp and lower jaw, the fangs audibly clicking as they connected to bone. The utahraptor writhed and screeched, kicking blindly until its scything talons dragged out the rest of the kaprosuchus's innards.

The kaprosuchus was disemboweled in seconds.

Andrei remained within the mangrove roots as he watched the kaprosuchus turn to dead-weight atop the utahraptor. The utahraptor rolled beneath the kaprosuchus, attempting to buck the dead animal, but with little success. The kaprosuchus's jaws were still locked around the utahraptor's head. From what Andrei could tell, the utahraptor might not survive the night.

The utahraptor began to wail, and Andrei's eyes widened upon the recognition of the screams that had filled so many of his nights with insomniac terror. In less than a minute, three more utahraptors materialized within the mist. Andrei returned the Makarov to his temple as he waited for the predators to leave.

The three utahraptors gnawed and kicked at the kaprosuchus's neck until the head was completely severed from the rest of its body. The injured utahraptor managed to climb to its feet, but the kaprosuchus's jaws were still mounted to its head. The injured utahraptor laid on the ground, and with a well-placed kick from another utahraptor, the kaprosuchus head was sent rolling.

The crackling of the kaprosuchus teeth breaking off were succeeded by the pained screams of the injured utahraptor. While the kaprosuchus head had been

[8]

removed, several of the broken tusks had been left embedded in the injured utahraptor's scalp and lower jaw. The injured utahraptor sat in the center of its pack, panting and wheezing with exhaustion. Blood spilled from the utahraptor's whimpering jaws like crimson oil.

Andrei remained where he had fallen beside the mangrove long after the utahraptors had abandoned the mangal forest. The silence that had pervaded left with the dromaeosaurids. The volume of insects buzzing and sizzling from the canopy was slowly returned to normal levels, and birds began to chirrup as they hunted for fish and crab along the river. Before tending to his wounds from the kaprosuchus, Andrei thought of a name for the injured utahraptor that had accidentally saved his life.

Sobek; the Nihil River God.

CONQUEST OF CANAAN

Vietnam, 1970.

The arrival of the helicopter was muted by a monsoon.

General Amadeus Jericho of the US Armed Forces was bent crooked over his mahogany desk, a cigar bobbing between his pinched scowl. He was a relic of the WWII-era gung-ho leadership sensibilities that had once crafted the likes of Patton and MacArthur. Jericho's patriarchal eyes leered forth from a plateau brow, his wrinkles disguised stress as wisdom. His frame was still trim and limber beneath a tightly starched olive-drab uniform. Jericho's well-crafted persona had served him well within the ranks of the pentagon.

Jericho grumbled in distaste as he shuffled through field reports signed by Doctor Andrei Wynn and Captain Xavier Wise of Stalker Force. They were the same usual boring dredge; dinosaur migration patterns, newly discovered nesting sites, population counts spread across bell-curve graphs that were nauseating to skim through.

Jericho signed every dotted line, tucked them all away in manila folders, and buried them within the slush pile that lined the back wall of his office. He checked his Rolex; CIA agents sent by the Pentagon would arrive to whisk away the slush pile within the hour.

Jericho chewed on the stem of his cigar as he thumbed through his desk drawer for a bottle of bourbon. He tugged on the cork, grunting with effort until the bottle finally released with an enervating *pop*. Jericho plucked the cigar from his lips and put the bottle in its place, tilting his head back to drain a long pull of fire down

[10]

his throat. The vigor of the liquor momentarily washed away the clutter from the fifty-plus year old general's mind.

A year had passed since the destruction of the Russian compound that had once occupied Jericho's career. General Amadeus Jericho had once been notorious for spear-heading innumerous clandestine operations within Vietnam. He had seen the tenacity of the Viet Cong guerillas and doubled down on fighting fire with fire. Jericho's forces had been responsible for reaping the majority of classified intel from the Vietnamese landscape. The NVA was routinely subverted by his ingenious strategies and his men slaughtered the Viet Cong in droves like livestock. All of his hard work, his borderline sociopathic sense of control, and the men he had hand-selected for service had culminated in the discovery of the Russian compound.

It was a long-known fact that the Soviet Union maintained a presence in the shadows of Northern Vietnam, but the Russian compound was an entirely new beast to tame. Back-tracking radioactive shipments of Polonium-T had led Jericho's men to an isolated jungle valley far north of the Demilitarized Zone that separated North and South Vietnam. When Jericho pinpointed the long-rumored construct, he immediately planted a base within the same valley and dedicated the next year of his service to understanding what the Russians were doing.

A year of intelligence-gathering had rendered very little in the face of an indomitable environment. The teams of Green Beret and Army Rangers that probed the forests beyond the perimeter fences of the base scarcely returned. The paltry Viet Cong presence hadn't been to blame for the loss of American lives, nor were the Russians working in secrecy at the most northern-point of the valley. After dispatching the infamous search and rescue team known as Vulture Squad, the answers to Jericho's endless questions finally became clear.

[11]

The valley was plagued with dinosaurs.

A Russian particle accelerator known as the 'Collider' had inadvertently triggered a wormhole, a rip in the fabric of space-time. The wormhole, while temporary, had dispensed a countless menagerie of prehistoric creatures into the local ecosystem in the blink of an eye. The Russians had largely left the dinosaurs alone up until their base was destroyed by a pair of Tyrannosaurus rex. Upon seizing control of the valley and reporting back to the Pentagon, Jericho had been horrified to hear the decree from statesmen on high.

The dinosaurs were to be preserved.

Jericho tucked the bourbon bottle back into his desk and returned the cigar to its chapped-lip mantle. Jericho leaned over his desk and started writing correspondence to the commanders of the nearest American bases beyond the valley. Jericho's personal black ops team, the Hyenas, routinely investigated infantry reports of 'large, feathered animals', 'unidentified hostile wildlife', and the occasional accurate identification of 'dinosaurs'. Quarantining the dinosaurs had proven to be too great a task, ultimately taking the Army Corps of Engineers nearly the entirety of the year to build following the destruction of the Russian compound.

The migration had already begun.

Jericho heard the door to his office swing open, the rush of cascading rainfall masking the footsteps of men shuffling into his musty hovel. He didn't even bother to look up from his paperwork. It took one of the men the act of clearing his throat for Jericho to drag his eyes away from the documents that littered his desk.

"What," Jericho grunted; a statement rather than a question.

Jericho's eyes widened when he registered the pair of black-suited men standing before him. The larger of the pair was a stocky man in his late forties, his sand-blonde hair neatly trimmed. The forty-year old's face was non-descript, a semblance of any uncle dragged from a Texan barbeque. Jericho shot up from his chair and extended a hand to the agent.

"Sorry," Jericho muttered awkwardly. "How was the flight?"

"Like riding the id," the older agent said. "All bucking, no bull. Shinoda here's still dealing with his first bout of air-sickness. Kid's never been on a huey before; virgin's flight is over an active fucking war-zone."

Shinoda, the shorter of the pair, appeared to Jericho to be in his late twenties. The young Asian American's white button-up shirt was soaked with a mixture of sweat and rain. He stood by the door, his forehead pressed against the wall and a hand on his gut.

"I've read his file," Jericho said. He looked at the older agent. "And you're Russell Simmons?"

"Yeah, sorry to show up before the scheduled time, but I figured it would be the best for both of us not to waste the Agency's time stalling this meeting any further."

Russell took Jericho's hand and shook it firmly.

"So, Stalker Force?"

[13]

After a round of brandy and cheap cigars, Jericho led Russell and Shinoda through the pounding monsoon to the Stalker Force war-room. The sun found little foothold within the concrete curtain of cloud cover. Every color but a grey gradient had been washed from the sky. The base had been built atop a low hill in the southern end of the valley, and the Army Corps of Engineers had filled the red-dirt clearing with enough buildings to house a small village.

Jericho shepherded the CIA agents past the wooden cabins that served as the barracks for his men, around the newly-built helipad, and into a freshly made ebony-wood cabin. The skunk-fire smell of marijuana reached Jericho's nose as soon as they entered the weather-beaten building. Jericho forced a smile for Shinoda and Russell; *surely* he couldn't have known what most of the soldiers under his command were doing in their down time.

"Xavier, Andrei, look sharp," Jericho said. "We have company."

Xavier Wise, the Captain of Stalker Force, rose from a desk positioned against the right-hand wall of the war-room. Xavier was a few years shy of thirty, dressed in well-worn tiger stripe fatigues that clung tightly to his athletic frame. He saluted to Jericho, then lowered his hand and nodded to the pair of civilians behind the old general.

"Do the suits have names?" Xavier asked in a dry monotone.

"Russell Simmons, CIA," Russell said, stepping forward. He had his hand stretched out for Xavier to take, but Xavier merely eyed it like a raw steak that had been dropped on the floor.

Xavier's eyes darted to Shinoda.

"Are you CIA too?" Xavier grunted.

[14]

"Unfortunately," Shinoda smiled. "My brother was the foot-soldier."

"Bishop," Jericho sighed, shaking his head. "He'll be missed."

Xavier eyed the two men warily. He looked across the room to where Andrei Wynn was lying on a cot, frantically sketching in a leather-bound journal. Xavier whistled and Andrei looked up from his illustrations to the unfamiliar men flanking Jericho. Andrei quickly shut the notebook and made a bee-line to the ensemble.

"Doctor Wynn," Andrei said, extending a hand to Russell first, then to Shinoda. "You're with the Central Intelligence Agency, *dah*?"

"That's right," Jericho said. "Tell 'em about your research."

Andrei vigorously waved for the men to follow him to Xavier's desk. There was a dusty old utahraptor skull lying on the table with a freshly polished ka-bar resting through its orbital sockets. A topographical map of Vietnam was spread beneath the utahraptor skull like a tablecloth, with bright red lines tracking the hypothetical passage of different dinosaur species to localized sightings beyond the valley. Andrei took a revolver off of the map, tucked it in his holster, and withdrew a smoldering cigarette from an ashtray beside the skull.

"The utahraptors are our biggest concerns," Andrei said. He took his journal and flipped it open, revealing penciled illustrations of a utahraptor with broken tusks protruding from its scalp. He tapped the regal animal lying in repose with his finger as he exhaled a cotton ball of cigarette smoke.

"There were originally two colonies of utahraptors in the Valley; Xavier and I call the larger colony 'Cyclops Colony', and the smaller colony is 'Sobek Colony'. Cyclops Colony left after the destruction of the USSR's collider."

[15]

Andrei pointed to a smaller, hand-drawn map of the valley tacked to a board behind the desk. He traced a small circle at the northern portion of the valley, just outside of where the Russian compound had once stood.

"Xavier and I believe that Cyclops Colony left because of the death of their Alpha male. Perhaps the explosion that destroyed the compound urged them to evade any human presence; the entire colony left, and we still have no idea where the hell they've ended up. The colony seems to have split up and gone off in different families, as far as the sightings claim."

"Really though, *Cyclops* Colony?" Shinoda asked, smirking. "What kind of name is that? Are you really into Homer's *Odyssey*, or is there something I'm not getting here?"

Andrei pointed to an illustration pinned to the board above the desk. The drawing showed a full-grown utahraptor mid-sprint, the long jaws opened in a scream, blood flying from its serrated fangs. A ka-bar was planted firmly in its eye socket.

"We think Cyclops, the alpha male, killed Bishop," Andrei said gravely. "Or maybe one of his pack-mates."

Shinoda cleared his throat, stroking his blood-hued tie with one hand. His eyes fell upon the utahraptor skull lying on the desk. He gently prodded the dagger resting in the eye sockets, as if testing the bones for a reaction.

"Don't worry," Xavier grunted. "He doesn't bite…anymore."

Shinoda paced away silently as Andrei directed the room's attention to the illustration of Sobek the utahraptor.

[16]

"Sobek Colony is the utahraptor colony that is still remaining in the valley," Andrei said, pointing to the tusk-crowned dromaeosaurid. "This is the alpha male, the one we named the Colony after. There have been innumerous utahraptor families – selective individuals vying for individual survival rather than collective – leaving Sobek Colony to escape the valley. Some of these opportunistic families have taken to attacking the Army engineers that do regular maintenance on the perimeter. Considering the size of some of the local wildlife, it's a regular job, and one that frequently ends in missing engineers."

"Even with Stalker Force's supervision?" Russell asked, glancing at Jericho.

"Unfortunately," Xavier spoke up. He pointed to three other illustrations pinned to the board. One was clearly a feathered Tyrannosaurus, with the caption 'The Father' scrawled in the corner. The others were theropods largely unfamiliar with the civilian populace; Cryolophosaurus and Yutyrannus.

"In most ecosystems, the food chain is kept in balance by a kind of caloric pyramid," Xavier said. "Producers like plants are at the bottom, then herbivores above that, predators further up, and finally the apex predators at the very top. The higher up the pyramid, the less caloric intake is available to the species in that upper range, and the lower the population count."

"Can you sum it up in one sentence?" Russell asked.

Xavier and Andrei exchanged stoic eye contact.

"Sure," Xavier grunted. "There's too many predatory dinosaurs to share a mutual food source, so starving utahraptors have been hunting humans opportunistically, like a tiger with broken teeth and nothing to lose."

[17]

"The utahraptors aren't necessarily the biggest threat, however," Andrei said, looking to Jericho and Russell. "We've observed large populations of birds dying for no discernible reason. We think it may be connected to diseases carried by the dromaeosaurid dinosaurs, namely Utahraptor and Deinonychus, but we don't have the proper resources to determine it."

"Your PhD is a resource," Jericho grunted.

"A PhD that isn't in microbiology," Andrei said, narrowing his eyes.

"Don't worry, we're going to take care of it," Russell said, resting a hand on the utahraptor skull. "Once you have this 'Sobek Colony' eliminated, we can set up proper research stations here to study the effects the dinosaurs are having on the native ecosystem. Until then, it's far too dangerous for us to invest resources into. We've already pooled enough taxpayer money getting y'all to *this* point."

"Studying the effects of dinosaurs in a research station," Andrei grumbled. "I feel like I may have heard that proposition, but I've been wrong before."

"So where do you think Sobek Colony is now?" Russell asked.

"We believe they've taken up residence in the Cyclops Colony's old nesting site," Xavier said, pointing to a circled portion of the map marked as 'Nesting Site A'. "We've been tracking their footprints for months, and they all seem to lead here. It's a perfect place; there's no more humans in that section of the valley, there's a more diverse food supply thanks to the waterfall, and there's a T. rex nest that keeps all other competition far away."

"When are you going to investigate the nest?" Russell asked.

[18]

"Tonight," Jericho grunted. "As soon as Stalker Force quits playing around in the armory."

"Gotta stay armed and ready," Xavier winked; a brief twitch. "Did you need anything else?"

"No, that'll be all," Russell said. "C'mon, Shinoda."

Shinoda had been struck slack-jawed at the sight of three taxidermied heads mounted to the wall beside the desk. One was a kaprosuchus, with tusks protruding nearly six inches from its tightly clamped jaws. Beneath it were the heads of a stygimoloch, a herbivore with a parrot's beak and a domed skull lined with razor-sharp protrusions, and a deinonychus, a smaller relative of utahraptor with a head roughly the size of a wolf's, replete with glistening blue-black feathers and a reptilian turquoise snout.

"You like 'em?" Xavier called out to Shinoda. "Mounted 'em myself."

Shinoda tore his eyes away from the marbles glistening in the deinonychus's eye sockets. He quickly followed Russell and Jericho out of the war-room and into the storm. They remained silent until they finally reached the huey awaiting them on the helipad. Shinoda climbed into the cabin while Russell remained with Jericho in the pummeling tempest.

"You're doing fine, Jericho," Russell said. "Damn fine. All the boys at the Pentagon that are in 'The Know' are rooting for you. They think it's going to be a lot more palpable for the folks back home if we're in Vietnam for dinosaur research rather than…everything else."

"You're going to take the news to the public?" Jericho asked.

Russell waved a hand dismissively.

"We're going to let the war correspondents handle that one," Russell said. "It's only a matter of time, anyhow. With all these different dinosaurs popping up all over south-east Asia, the good American people will be privy to the classified intel in no time."

Russell spread his arms wide, as if to illustrate the scope of possibilities.

"Won't that be fun?" Russell said. "Just imagine the reactions back home. The words 'Stalker Force' and 'General Jericho' will be on everybody's lips. Y'all will be the first men to officially discover *living dinosaurs*. I wouldn't be the least bit shocked if a movie gets made out of all this."

"Keep dreaming," Jericho coughed.

"In the mean time, we have a small favor to ask," Russell said. He withdrew an envelope from his breast pocket and handed it to Jericho. "The Pentagon is collaborating with an exciting new contractor called 'KrishnaKane Corps', or 'KKC'. The boys in the Pentagon are interested in what went wrong with the Collider back at the Russian Compound. If you can get your Hyenas digging up some fresh intel, I can promise you a job more suitable to your tastes."

Jericho took the envelope. When he opened it, a thick green wad of American currency blossomed in the rain. Jericho quickly pushed the bills back into the envelope and tucked it in his jacket pocket.

"That compound's by that Sobek Colony, right?" Russell said. "You could probably fly in Stalker Force for some work and have your Hyenas digging up the dirt right across the way. Kill two birds with one stone. Sound good?"

[20]

"Sounds promising," Jericho smiled. He saluted as Russell entered the huey.

"Happy hunting," Russell called over his shoulder, shutting the cabin door.

Jericho watched as the huey lifted off of the helipad and rose into the cloud cover, the waning search light blossoming forth through the mist before finally being swallowed entirely within the Vietnamese monsoon. Jericho put a hand down in his pocket, feeling the slightly dampened fifty-grand bundle within the envelope. He wasn't sure what new position awaited him with the destruction of Sobek Colony, but it had to be better than this.

Anything was better than the hunting of Stalker Force.

TYRANT FATHER

A tremendous thunderstorm thrashed through the valley like a runaway bull, shearing apart the tree tops that draped the mountain walls. Xavier Wise and Andrei Wynn were each thankful for the shelter the elder kapok trees provided from the full force of the biting rain. The rest of their team, the first members of Stalker Force, was gathered around the pair with their rifles fixed on their shifting rain-swept surroundings. Nightfall had struck with the force of a monsoon, and their hunting quarry was most adept when man's senses failed.

It had been over a year since the men of Vulture Squad first set foot in the infamous valley festering with dinosaurs. After the surviving members of Vulture Squad parted ways, Xavier Wise had been assigned by General Jericho to personally track the dinosaurs of the valley with the assistance of Doctor Wynn. Xavier had been given free rein to select the best men possible for the job, regardless of service branch or prior expertise.

Xavier knew his mission was one that required men that were capable of thinking outside of the box that military training often caged the minds of men within. He wanted men that were more than just Special Forces or bloodthirsty; Xavier wanted warriors, hunters, and battle-tested survivors. His search had taken him across all echelons of the American military, but his efforts had been well rewarded.

The first man that Xavier had recruited into Stalker Force was Syd Kinane, an M60 operator and Xavier's second in command. He was a mountain of a man, a colossus with the build of a silverback and an alpha ego to match. Xavier had first met Syd Kinane during an operation with Vulture Squad, when they had retrieved Syd and several of his platoon-mates from a Viet Cong internment camp.

When Xavier first met Syd, the burly goliath had been half of his current weight and nearly feral from a year spent in a holding pen no bigger than a dog kennel. Syd's indomitable spirit and endless defiance had made him into a prime pincushion for the Viet Cong interrogators. At the time of his liberation, Syd had told Xavier that he and his squad-mates were Army Rangers caught during a routine patrol. The truth of Syd's past had been washed away by black ink; his involvement with Tiger Force remained in the shadows like so many other military disasters.

Syd sauntered through the storm beside Xavier, the M60 heavy machine gun hanging like an axe in his thick-knuckled grip. His arms were as thick as the boughs of a ficus, the sleeves of his jacket torn away to expose stick-and-poke tattoos bestowed by old friends from Los Angeles. A blonde handlebar moustache hung limply from his permanent scow l. The locks of golden hair that spilled out from under his helmet were worthy of Samson and Delilah's adoration.

James Molnar, the close-quarters specialist, walked close behind Syd. Molnar was a stout, stocky man with a sparkling-bald dome. His eyes always seemed to be narrowed in a lecherous leer, barely emerging from above his sharply curved and bent nose. The Remington shotgun that he carried was covered in white lettering from more languages than Xavier or Andrei could dream to decipher. They were mantras from around the world, pulled from texts like the *Bhardo Thodal* and the *Lesser Key of Solomon*.

Xavier had met Molnar during an R&R break in Saigon. They had ordered drinks at the same time in a decrepit bar within the city's greasy heart of alleyways and incense-choked brothels. Xavier had recognized the book in Molnar's hand – *Hell's Angels* by Hunter S Thompson – and the pair immediately connected over a night of gonzo reminiscing. When Xavier later discovered

[23]

Molnar was an accomplished martial-artist and former para-jumper, he seized the opportunity and brought the renegade pseudo-psychonaut into Stalker Force.

Konnor Jung, the medic of Stalker Force, was walking beside Andrei Wynn. He was a descendant of Japanese immigrants, a first-generation American raised in an internment camp outside of Tule Lake. Konnor had originally served with Xavier in the Green Beret before Xavier had been selected for Vulture Squad. Konnor had been something of an apprentice to Xavier, and his cool demeanor reminded Xavier of the calm he once felt within himself before he had discovered the presence of modern-day dinosaurs.

Dinosaur-related injuries required a cool head like Konnor Jung.

The rest of Stalker Force, the sniper-spotter duo, trailed behind the team through the drenched undergrowth. Michael Waters and Craig Jacobs were an unsightly pair; Michael was a stocky young African American man whereas Craig was a rotund, bearded thirty-year old. Craig and Michael had assisted Xavier and Andrei during their first recon into the valley before Stalker Force had even been conceived of.

Michael Waters had been raised in a small town on the outskirts of Cincinnati, Ohio. His upbringing had been meager, and his adolescence had been a gauntlet through relentless street fights and crack-head robberies. Michael's inherent ability to remain unperturbed to bullets slinging by his scalp had been fostered throughout his high-school years. The peace he found within the concrete fields of violence had allowed him to become one of the greatest snipers the Army had ever acquired.

Craig Jacobs, however, was a well-read and highly perceptive former Green Beret. After half of a decade spent in the brush, he no longer felt the familiar

[24]

fangs of paranoia most troops were crippled by. Craig's fears were exorcised through the endless letters he wrote to his wife and their newborn son. He was the oldest member of Stalker Force, and he looked the part. Craig's skin had been sketched upon by bayonets, bullets, daggers, and the teeth and talons of the jungles he had found himself in with the Green Beret.

Xavier suppressed a grin as the men of Stalker Force walked in formation around himself and Andrei. With Syd on point, Konnor and Molnar guarding their flanks, Michael and Craig watching their backs, the team was complete and in synchronicity. During a previous excursion into the valley, Xavier and Andrei had finally tracked down the nesting site of Sobek Colony.

The utahraptors were the true apex predators of the valley. Humans were little more than intelligent prey to the cunning dromaeosaurids. At almost ten feet tall, twenty feet long, and a metric ton in weight, the utahraptors were rarely challenged by the other carnivorous megafauna in the valley. Xavier and Andrei had witnessed the utahraptors going talon-for-talon with even the quetzalcoatlus and the Father T. rex, the largest predator presently walking the earth.

With so little natural competition to prevent the spread of the utahraptor population, it was up to Stalker Force to track and kill the stealthy dromaeosaurids. So far, Xavier and Andrei's early excursions into the valley had revealed startlingly little evidence of the utahraptors. General Jericho kept hammering the mission statement into their skulls via the radio; *find and kill the utahraptors. They should all be destroyed.*

Xavier and Andrei's first expedition without Stalker Force had amounted to the discovery of three utahraptor nesting sites; two small family-sized nests on the south-end of the valley, nestled within the opposing mountain walls, as well as a

[25]

third nest in the deepest basin at the northern end. With little to show for the two southern nesting sites, Xavier rallied Stalker Force to track the passage of the utahraptors from the abandoned northern nesting site, known as Nest Site A.

While Xavier and Stalker Force were searching for their quarry through the jungle, the Army Corps of Engineers were busy repairing the concrete perimeter that penned in the less cunning inhabitants of the valley. It was of the utmost importance for Xavier and Stalker Force to find the remaining utahraptors before they could wreak further havoc on the construction crews. There were too many men vanishing in the night, too many bloody trails leading further into the depths of the jungle.

Xavier had spent months preparing for this moment.

The passage of Stalker Force was disguised audibly by the relentless onslaught of rain crashing against the upper canopy. Xavier understood that if he could scarcely see or hear, that meant the utahraptors, as well as the other carnivores in the valley, were at the advantage. He had made the decision to follow the utahraptor tracks for another hundred meters, or until they were no longer distinguishable from the layers of rotting leaf litter.

Xavier led Stalker Force through the jungle and into a grove of bamboo. There was scarcely any undergrowth beneath the countless columns of green vertebrae. As Xavier made his way downhill, he caught sight of a lone clearing at the bottom of the basin. In a brief glare of lightning, a gargantuan theropod was revealed slumbering in the center of a forty-foot wide nest. The light was vanquished as quickly as it had appeared, and the details of the sleeping dinosaur were lost to the shadows.

Xavier raised a fist for the others to see; a sign to stop. The men of Stalker Force crouched beneath the pillars of bamboo as Xavier unfolded a map on the soggy carpet of leaf litter.

Andrei leaned over Xavier's shoulder and shined a penlight onto the heavily-creased laminated parchment. Obese water droplets burst against the topographical lines denoting the features of the valley. Xavier traced Stalker Force's journey across the landscape with his index finger, smearing the raindrops towards the nest of the Tyrannosaurus family.

"I think we've been tricked by the birds," Xavier mumbled.

Andrei groaned. "What a shock-"

Andrei was interrupted by a bolt of lightning that tore the black skies above the bamboo asunder. The gargantuan body of the sleeping Mother T. rex briefly glimmered in the dazzling light. Rust-brown leather skin glittered in the flickering strobe, and the tyrannosaur's robust chest swelled with a mighty yawn. Rain cascaded over the lumpy ridge of bone above the Mother's snout. If the Mother was sleeping with her chicks, that meant the Father was somewhere nearby, potentially on the hunt.

"It's a fucking rex," Michael, the sniper, whispered. "It's real."

"Of course it's real," Andrei said, shooting a dirty look over his shoulder. "Why do you think we're here?"

"To find raptor nests," Craig, Michael's spotter, muttered. "Not a rex."

"What should we do?" Konnor, the medic, asked.

Xavier stared at the Mother T. rex. His eyes ran circles around the sleeping theropod's curled, shadow-swathed body. Even though she was at the bottom of a hill and sleeping alone in an expansive clearing, the female tyrannosaur appeared to be large enough to move mountains. Xavier faintly wished the Mother's sole infant wouldn't wake up, but more so than that, he hoped the Father wouldn't return home so soon.

The storm made Xavier think otherwise.

"Alright guys, we need to turn around and head back the way we came," Xavier said to the rest of Stalker Force. Luckily, the rain and wind concealed his voice from the sleeping Mother T. rex. "If we head back to Nest Site A, we can call Ricardo for our evac and set up a perimeter. Since the utahraptors abandoned the nest, I doubt any other predators will be coming back to it."

The men agreed to Xavier's plan, nodding in silence.

The storm filled the silence for Stalker Force. They half-jogged, half-sprinted through the ivy-tangled bamboo rods. The rain crawled over their bodies, soaking through their uniforms to the skin with an icy bite. Xavier and Andrei remained in the center of the group as they ran.

Andrei kept his head low, fervently examining the shifting silhouettes of the forest. Xavier held his encroaching panic at bay, using the adrenaline it provided as fuel for his tired legs.

A spear of electricity sliced through the sky above the canopy, illuminating the bulging, leprous thunderclouds. White light snapped through the creases in the tree tops. Xavier jerked his head up – a reaction to the scream of lightning – and caught a glimpse of a silhouetted theropod at the top of the hill they were climbing.

[28]

The towering bipedal dinosaur was draped in robes of darkness, quill-like pre-feathers forming a mane around his throat and scalp.

The Father T. rex was returning to his nest.

Xavier saw the silhouetted goliath looming overhead and immediately dropped to the forest floor. The rest of the team, in a show of instinctual pack mentality, dropped down beside him a second later. Andrei, however, stumbled forward and spilled over Konnor Jung.

The luminescent flare of lightning was vanquished with the concussive crash of colliding thunderclouds. The forest rolled around the men, frenzied shadows shifting through the rain-lashed understory. The shape of the Father T. rex was lost in the abysmal dark of the bamboo forest. Only the tyrannosaur's eyes remained visible; neon black orbs crackling with moonlight and mounting rage. Xavier could already hear the Father T. rex making its way down the sloping hillside, crushing saturated bamboo reeds to paste beneath its splayed feet.

Xavier chewed on his lip, counting the seconds until the Father T. rex would cross his path. He listened to the bamboo clatter and sway, the percussion of the storm playing through the shifting canopy. He didn't think the tyrannosaurus could see or hear the men in the dark, but if its olfactory senses were as keen as Andrei had previously proposed, the men were going to be a quick and easy meal for the apex predator.

The ground shuddered beneath Xavier's fingertips.

Xavier's eyes climbed from the earth to the sky as the Father T. rex's foul musk washed over his prone body. A deep chill cut through Xavier's core. His knees were trembling against the forest floor, churning deeper into the decaying leaves and

[29]

mud. The rest of the men surrounding Xavier and Andrei were hunched over, cowering in the darkness. They were painfully exposed in the sparse undergrowth.

Syd, Xavier's second in command, had one hand on his M60 and the other digging into the malleable turf. He planted his boots into the soil, arching his spine for a quick sprint. Xavier locked eyes with him and nodded. Syd accepted the cue and lunged forward, darting past the Father T. rex while the theropod was distracted by the biting rain and rustling canopy.

Xavier raised his head to watch Syd's silhouette vanish amongst the bamboo. A fat globule of saliva, thick as crude oil, slapped the crown of Xavier's scalp. He immediately flinched, but otherwise maintained his icy composure. When he dared to look up, he found himself staring at the Father T. rex's freshly-molted throat wattle. The flesh that hung from the tyrannosaur's barren throat bulged and writhed like tumors cloaked in scrotal skin. Fresh-grown pin feathers covered the Father T. rex's entire body like bone-white porcupine quills.

Xavier and Andrei both understood that molting meant the Father T. rex, like other birds, had just been through a breeding season. Xavier understood that most large animals experienced a kind of rut during mating season; a state of hormonal rage. A male tyrannosaurus in the throes of a rut, or in *musth* like an elephant, would be an unstoppable engine of destruction.

More so than usual, Xavier thought.

Thinking fast, Xavier used a series of hand gestures to direct Molnar, the CQB specialist, to move around the right flank of the Father T. rex, and for Craig and Michael to move left. The three men crawled prone through the saturated leaf litter, around the Father T. rex's taloned feet, and into the darkness beyond the tip of

[30]

its tail. Only Xavier, Konnor, and Andrei remained beneath the Father T. rex's slowly-chugging chest.

The Father T. rex had lost Stalker Force in the rain.

Xavier was attempting osmosis with the forest floor, sinking deeper into the festering soil as the Father T. rex's snout bobbed through the air a meter above his back. The tyrannosaurus opened its jaws, revealing a maw of chipped and bloodied fangs that framed a throbbing gullet. The Father T. rex's fat, forked tongue heaved out from between its jaws and flapped through the rain around Xavier's face. Xavier bit down on his lip, clenching his eyes shut as the tyrannosaur's fetid jaws drew closer. The tongue brushed sickly-warm spit along Xavier's cheeks, probing for soft flesh...

A flare was popped from several dozen meters behind the Father T. rex. The tyrannosaur grunted in surprise at the sudden hiss of spitting sparks and turned to face its new territorial adversary. Vermillion light, hazy with smoke, burned forth through the dark space between the silhouetted beams of bamboo.

While the Father T. rex was distracted by the flare, cocking his bulbous quill-coated skull, Xavier slapped Konnor on the back and directed him away from the tyrannosaur. Konnor dragged Andrei out from under the Father T. rex and the two men hustled off to the rest of the team. Xavier was left alone beneath the disgruntled tyrant. Xavier could recognize the distinction between the rustling of vegetation and the movement of Stalker Force. The rest of Stalker Force was crawling away from the flare, back to Xavier.

Xavier pleaded with his medulla oblongata for action; he had to move, or else the Father T. rex would find him and the others. The loss of prior members of Vulture Squad still haunted Xavier's subconscious, and his mind had been plagued

[31]

by their screams for a year of anguished mental isolation. Xavier refused to lose his new squad-mates, even if it meant sacrificing his own life.

Xavier studied the quills quivering across the Father T. rex's throat.

T. rex's mate for life; the Father would understand loss.

Xavier leapt to his feet and pivoted away from the Father T. rex, sprinting towards its nest. The Father T. rex turned from the flare and bellowed at Xavier's backside, causing him to stumble. Xavier found his footing as the Father T. rex's feet pounded downhill towards him.

Xavier was flailing through the bamboo, shouldering past the hardened swaying pillars, his hands slipping as they brushed past slick fiber. He was blind in the rain, the Father T. rex's panting breath filling his mental void. His sense of urgency was immense; he only hoped the other men of Stalker Force weren't foolish enough to follow him.

Moonlight ebbed through a break in the canopy; a contraction of lightning above revealed the slumbering Mother T. rex in the center of the basin below. Xavier hit a hard left as the splash of light was relinquished, and the Father T. rex stampeded past. Xavier held his breath; he was upwind of the Father T. rex. The aggravated carnivore barreled down the slope and slowed to a trot as he approached his mate and their sole infant. The Mother T. rex was already rousing from her slumber, groaning as she blinked groggily at the enraged Father.

The rest of Stalker Force crawled to Xavier and settled on their haunches around him. Xavier was still staring wide-eyed into the darkness where only the eyes of the tyrannosaurs were visible; spectral lights bobbing and drifting through the glistening black rainfall. Stalker Force was silent as they listened to the theropods

[32]

chortle and whinny through their prickly throat sacs. It took a nudge from Andrei for Xavier to realize he was surrounded.

"Good thinking," Andrei muttered. "Maybe a heads-up next time, *dah*?"

"Tyrannosaurs mate for life," Xavier mumbled from the bottom of his throat. "All I had to do was remind him what was important; protecting his brood."

"Clever," Andrei said. "Like Sobek."

Xavier frowned, fixing his lips in thought as the tyrannosaurs roared.

"We'll need to figure that one out," Xavier said. "But first, we need that evac."

"Where were you thinking, boss?" Syd asked. "Nest-Site A?"

"No," Xavier said, shaking his head. "There could be another ambush waiting for us, for all we know. We need to call an evac from the biggest clearing this section of the valley."

Andrei stared at Xavier. The thunderclouds clapped approvingly.

"No," Andrei said, shaking his head. "We said we'd never go back there."

"Where?" Molnar asked. "We're in a valley of dinosaurs; what difference does any other place make?"

Andrei sighed and wiped the rain from his glasses. He couldn't clear out the condensation, so he grunted and gave up, tossing his hands up in defeat.

"The Ashtray," Andrei stated. "The Russian compound."

[33]

TYRANT FATHER II

What remained of the Russian compound after the destruction of the second collider had been returned to the hungry forests of Vietnam. The building that had once housed the collider had been obliterated in a massive explosion. The piles of rubble where the building had once stood were covered in leafy ivies, resembling obtuse green mounds dotting the compound's muddy clearing. The perimeter walls, once standing as a twenty-foot high ring of mortar and steel, had been thrown by the detonation into the surrounding forest. Some of the crumbling concrete sheets were still standing, leaning against the monolithic durians and kapok trees and ensnared by python-thick vines.

Nguyen Con Giáp observed the abandoned Russian compound with mild detachment. After being captured and liberated from Viet Cong guerillas with Charlie Miller, a former member of Vulture Squad, Nguyen had been dragged along by Vulture Squad to rescue General Jericho from the Russians that had controlled the valley at the time.

When Nguyen and Vulture Squad had originally arrived to the compound it had been in ruins, the mutilated bodies of the Russians scattered and masticated in the open clearing. Unbeknownst to Vulture Squad, the Father and Mother T. rex had slaughtered the Russians in the throes of parental rage. After escaping a colony of hungry and irate utahraptors, the remaining survivors of Vulture Squad – with the help of Andrei and Nguyen – destroyed the remnants of the Russian compound and their collider.

A year had passed, and in that time Nguyen had served as an honorary member of General Jericho's black ops team, the Hyenas. Despite the promotion into Jericho's most trusted ranks, Nguyen had felt nothing for his perceived success. He had expected General Jericho to send him on clandestine missions throughout Vietnam to stop the spread of communism and the Viet Cong, but since his inclusion into the Hyenas Nguyen had only been used as a tool for illicit operations. The villages in South Vietnam continued to fall like domino pieces, and Jericho continued to do nothing to halt the collapse of the democratic territories.

As Nguyen followed the other three members of his team, he attempted to bury the memories rising like ghosts from the detritus of the abandoned compound. When the Hyenas examined the destroyed remains of the collider, Nguyen had to subdue mental visions of Captain Baker of Vulture Squad wrestling with a monstrous one-eyed utahraptor nicknamed the 'Cyclops'.

When Nguyen and the Hyenas jogged through the rapacious rainfall to check out the still-standing pillbox bunkers, Nguyen tried to forget the smell of the Russian carcasses that had once seeped viscera and bodily fluids across the muddy clearing.

The traumatic memories would pass, but Nguyen's anger was unyielding.

The Hyenas had been sent into the valley without any notice being made to the members of Stalker Force. While Stalker Force investigated Utahraptor Nest-Site A, the Hyenas searched for any intel on the Collider that they could gather from the Russian compound. If any carnivores made trouble for the Hyenas, they could simply call in back-up from Xavier's nearby dinosaur hunters.

Jericho assumed that if they had Stalker Force in the area, an immediate evac could be negated. In the off chance that an immediate evac was necessary, the helicopter that had brought the Hyenas to the Russian compound was sitting at the ready on a nearby hill-top.

Nguyen had seen what the dinosaurs in the valley were capable of, and he wasn't sure if traveling on-foot without extra support was the wisest call for Jericho to make. Once again, Nguyen's pleas were ignored; as a rookie in the Hyenas and a Vietnamese native, his voice fell solely onto deaf ears.

Nguyen trailed at the rear of the Hyenas. Before the compound had been destroyed by Vulture Squad, all of the members of the prior black ops team had been killed by utahraptors. Jericho quickly assembled a trio from a rogues-gallery of military special forces recruits, men that fought viciously and killed indiscriminately for their status in the American military. They rejected Nguyen for his naivety, his inexperience; what good was a young Vietnamese man to the cruelest cut-throats the military had ever bred?

Nguyen was under the call-sign 'Panther', as a tribute to the former south-Vietnamese counter-guerilla troop that he had served with prior to joining the Hyenas. After the other Panthers had been murdered by Russian Spetsnaz, Nguyen carried the moniker into his new assignment. The other Hyenas went by the call-signs 'Scarecrow', 'Dutch', and 'Mr. Crowley'. Scarecrow was their Captain, guiding the others through the storm with a barrel-mounted flashlight.

All four Hyenas wore black battle fatigues bearing no insignias or patches; they couldn't give away any evidence to what nation they served. They were required to wear black balaclavas at all times; Nguyen personally detested the order, as it further dehumanized the men he was attempting to see as trust-worthy allies. With each clandestine mission, Nguyen saw the other Hyenas less as fellow purveyors of freedom and security and more of what they represented; the shadowy eyes, ears, and dagger of General Jericho.

[36]

Nguyen stumbled to a stop as Scarecrow raised his fist to halt the team. Their uniforms were quickly saturated by the rain as they stared at what remained of the former Russian general's lichen-camouflaged office. It was another pill-box bunker, but with a window beside the front door. Ferns and palm fronds had begun to bud and sprout from the soil around the bunker's trapezoid face. Scarecrow glanced at Nguyen and pointed at the scarred façade of the bunker.

"Look familiar?" Scarecrow asked, raising his voice to be heard through the pummeling rain.

Nguyen nodded. Mr. Crowley elbowed him.

"Speak, gook," Mr. Crowley grunted. "It's dark."

"Sorry," Nguyen said, narrowing his eyes. "Yes, sir."

Scarecrow nodded in the dark. He aimed the flashlight through the gaping doorway and ushered the others inside. Nguyen came inside last, after Scarecrow, and they began their search for intel. There was a desk decaying from mildew and rot in the center of the room and some moldy filing cabinets along the right-hand wall. Scarecrow, Dutch, and Mr. Crowley immediately pulled out pen-lights and started rifling through whatever documents they could find.

Nguyen was uneasy as he skimmed over the various documents in General Borodin's rotten mahogany desk. He was just starting to become fluent speaking English, but he had never seen the Russian alphabet before. After staring at a set of collider blueprints for a minute, Scarecrow ripped the sheet from Nguyen's hands and shoved him aggressively to the door.

Nguyen stumbled out of the room and into the storm. When he turned around, expecting to be accosted by Scarecrow, the door was slammed in his face.

[37]

The hinges gave way from exposure to rust and the door splashed into the mud, splattering Nguyen.

"Russian architecture," Dutch laughed from inside. "Go figure."

Nguyen shook his head and raised his M16A1. He kept the rifle to his cheek and scanned the overgrown perimeter for several minutes as the Hyenas inside the bunker shuffled through dissolving paperwork. Nguyen's arms began to teeter from holding the rifle up for so long, but he fought through the discomfort, the rain, the frustration, and allowed his anger to fuel him.

Jericho be damned, the Hyenas be damned, the entire valley be damned. All Nguyen wanted from life was to help his homeland, but even the most powerful nation in the world was willing to watch it fall for the sake of some dinosaurs and some Russian documents.

The ground began to tremble, and vibrations reverberated up through Nguyen's feet all the way to the crown of his skull. Nguyen began to feel disoriented, and he briefly lost his balance. The men inside of the bunker paused to listen to the rain.

Nguyen turned as Scarecrow stepped out into the wind-swept rainfall. Before Scarecrow could even speak, a resonant howl echoed throughout the valley, drowning the roaring monsoon. Scarecrow and Nguyen exchanged a nervous look through the eye-holes of their balaclavas as they listened to the roars of the distant behemoth blend and fade away within the rumbling of the storm.

"That's the big one," Scarecrow said. "Right?"

"Right," Nguyen nodded. He pulled out a field guide used by Stalker Force to identify the different species of dinosaurs in the valley, but Scarecrow took the book and shoved it back into Nguyen's rucksack.

"Put the book away," Scarecrow hissed. "Just tell me what the noise was."

"It was a T. rex," Nguyen said. "It might have been the Father-"

"Back to work, Panther," Scarecrow said, stepping back into the bunker. "Just keep an eye out and be ready to yell if that thing shows up."

Nguyen sighed as the heavy raindrops clawed at his uniform. He tried to wipe the water from his brow but got a calloused finger caught in his balaclava. Nguyen ripped the mask away with an irritated growl and tossed it across the clearing.

Nguyen briefly thought of Ryan Baker, the former captain of Vulture Squad, and he felt a pang in his chest. The screams of the Cyclops utahraptor echoed through the subconscious recesses of Nguyen's mind. Tremors returned to his fingers.

Or was that the T. rex?

Nguyen remained still as the ground rumbled beneath his feet. He could hear tree trunks creaking and cracking from beyond the collapsed perimeter walls, but was that just the winds of the monsoon pushing the kapoks to their breaking point? As a native son of Vietnam, Nguyen had witnessed the worst of his homeland's storms, and had long grown accustomed to the sound of ancient trees collapsing beneath the weight of weathering winds.

But this valley wasn't Nguyen's homeland; it was his country's cancer. That meant anything could lie in wait within the shadows of night. Nguyen was contemplating the desecration of his ancestral home when he heard a voice calling from the undergrowth beyond the broken concrete walls, a familiar voice echoing from the darkness of the jungle.

"Is that Nguyen?"

Nguyen narrowed his eyes as a flashlight beam cut across his face. As the beam fell from Nguyen's face, he saw a procession of human silhouettes surfacing from the jungle's pitch-black maw. The men were fast approaching, but even through the rain and shadow, Nguyen could make out the face of Xavier Wise leading the way into the clearing.

"Captain Wise?" Nguyen muttered, lowering the rifle.

Scarecrow stepped out of the office and stood beside Nguyen.

"What's all the noise, Panther?" Scarecrow asked. "You trying-"

When Scarecrow saw the approaching shapes of Stalker Force, he quickly shoved Nguyen aside and aimed his M14 rifle to the trespassers. Xavier Wise raised his M16A1 above his head as he came to a stop several meters from Nguyen and Scarecrow. The rest of Stalker Force stopped in their tracks, aiming their rifles at the masked aggressor standing beside Nguyen.

"Who the fuck are you?" Scarecrow barked. "Panther, hold your ground!"

"Nguyen, who the fuck is this guy?" Xavier asked, jerking his head towards Scarecrow. "What are you doing here?"

[40]

"I'll repeat," Scarecrow shouted, raising the M14 to Xavier's face. "Who are you?"

"Captain Wise, Stalker Force," Xavier said. "My arms are getting tired."

Scarecrow grunted and lowered his M14.

"What are you doing here?" Scarecrow asked. "Aren't you supposed to be digging through dinosaur shit?"

Dutch chuckled from the doorway. Mr. Crowley was watching as well.

"I was about to ask the same thing," Xavier said, cradling his rifle. "What are you doing here with Nguyen? Digging through Soviet shit for Jericho?"

"*Classified*," Scarecrow grunted. "Keep your nose in the dinosaur shit, Captain Wise."

"Smells like shit to me," Molnar grunted from behind Xavier.

"We need to call in an evac," Xavier said, scowling at Scarecrow. "Have you got a ride?"

Nguyen opened his mouth, but Scarecrow interrupted him.

"Not for you."

Xavier stared bullets through Scarecrow's pupils.

"Don't make me ask again," Xavier growled.

"We have an evac," Nguyen said. Scarecrow glared at him, but Nguyen ignored the frigid eyes on his back. "Our helicopter is up-hill. What's going on?"

[41]

"*Panther*," Scarecrow growled, tightening his grip on the M14.

"*Panther*," Andrei Wynn scoffed. "How cute. I forgot that Jericho likes to name his pets."

"Andrei," Xavier said, glancing at the scientist. "Not now."

"Can anybody tell me *what the fuck you're doing here*," Scarecrow snapped, shouting over the wind. "Jericho told us you were supposed to be tracking utahraptors at Site A; what the hell are you doing here? You're way off course."

There was a sudden *crack* from across the clearing, like an incredibly close bolt of lightning striking the earth. A towering durian tree collapsed into the clearing. The men flinched as the impact shook the ground beneath their feet. Mud was thrown through the air, splashing thick and viscous upon the soldiers. Xavier, Andrei, and Nguyen all turned at once towards the exposed root-ball of the fallen durian, half-concealed in the darkness.

Through the web of dirt-laden roots, the Father T. rex sighted his prey.

"Him," Xavier said, cocking a thumb back. "That's why."

TYRANT FATHER III

The Father T. rex was clearly agitated.

The pale eyes of the tyrannosaur drifted through the darkness along the perimeter of the Russian compound, occasionally vanishing as the theropod passed behind segments of the overgrown concrete wall. Even from across the clearing, Xavier could hear the carnivore huffing and snorting through the torrential downpour, its powerful feet sloshing through the meter-deep mud. Xavier was attempting to follow the tyrannosaur's warpath around the compound, but he was momentarily distracted when Dutch cleared his throat.

"What'd you do to piss 'm off?" Dutch asked.

"The utahraptors led us straight to his nest," Andrei said. He checked his watch and looked back to the pacing tyrannosaurus. "It's post-mating season, so he's probably working through the left-over testosterone Normally the Father wouldn't bother following us *this* far if he was simply chasing us out of his territorial range, but you see, Xavier here-"

"-Did what needed to be done," Xavier interjected, shooting a dirty look at Andrei. To the Hyenas he said, "Now would be a good time to call in that helicopter, if anybody was wondering."

"And do what," Scarecrow said. "Let that big fucker knock it around like a tin can? Nah, no bueno. I say we just wait it out until the big guy gets bored and leaves."

"*If* he leaves," Andrei grunted. "He has our scent; he knows we were in his territory. Xavier here ran right into his nest. How far away is the helicopter?"

"A minute's flight, an hour's walk," Scarecrow said, crossing his arms. "If you think we're about to hump it through this storm and bush to it, you're out of your fuckin' mind."

"I don't see a lot of options," Xavier said. "Either call it or start walking."

"Fuck it," Scarecrow said, turning away and waving a hand dismissively. "Start walking. We've got work to do."

Xavier stared at the back of Scarecrow's balaclava.

"You're serious?" Xavier asked incredulously. "Digging up dirt for Jericho is worth being around a tyrannosaurus rex?"

Scarecrow turned briefly, looked at Xavier, and shook his head.

"You better start walking, Captain."

Xavier glared at Scarecrow as he shuffled back into the Russian general's bunker with the rest of the Hyenas in tow. Xavier turned his back to the bunker and quickly scanned the perimeter for the spectral reflection of the Father T. rex's eyes. The tree-line was in a constant state of motion, and the unending rain turned every visible detail into a fluid blur. Steam escaped Xavier's lips in the form of a sigh. He looked over his shoulder to the rest of Stalker Force.

"C'mon," Xavier said. "I think we're good."

A heavy gust of wind threw syrup-thick saliva across Xavier's face. A sudden concussive roar from incredibly close crumpled his vertebrae and he fell back in shock. Xavier was practically swimming through the thick red clay as a second cataclysmic scream penetrated his skull. Stalker Force opened fire around him, and in the erratic muzzle-flare Xavier saw the Father T. rex rearing its head from behind the Russian general's bunker. The tyrannosaur put one foot on top of the weather-worn pillbox bunker and heaved its upper body halfway onto the structure.

"*Nguyen*," Xavier screamed to the pillbox. "*Get out of there!*"

The Hyenas started shouting as particles of cement drizzled onto their heads from the ceiling. Scarecrow grabbed a rucksack filled with collider blueprints and slung it over his shoulder, barking to the others, "*The intel, don't forget the intel*," as the Father T. rex howled and kicked the bunker from outside. Dutch stooped to pick up a journal of bio-weapons research just as the Father T. rex kicked a hole through the concrete wall behind him. The tyrannosaur's middle toe talon struck Dutch in the small of his back and sent him careening across the room, out the open door and tumbling into the storm.

"*Run*," Xavier screamed. "Stalker Force, *run*!"

Dutch was howling from where he had landed in the mud. Konnor dropped down beside him and flipped him over, revealing the gaping puncture wound that the Father T. rex's claw had created. It was as if Dutch had been hit by a shotgun; a deep pit was all that remained of his lower back, the lumbar visible and reduced to bony shrapnel in his exposed musculature tissue.

Konnor immediately knew that Dutch wouldn't survive.

"Get off of him," Scarecrow barked, kicking Konnor out of the way. He grabbed Dutch by the collar of his shirt and dragged him out into the rain with Mr. Crowley and Nguyen in tow. Dutch screamed the entire way, his paralyzed legs lolling limply through the mud. The bunker crumbled behind them as the Father T. rex delivered a final devastating kick to the façade.

[45]

Stalker Force and the Hyenas were exposed in the clearing.

"*The helicopter,*" Xavier screamed at Scarecrow. "*Where is it*?!"

"North West, 10'o clock," Scarecrow barked. "Lead the way!"

Xavier cursed under his breath as he sprinted to the tree-line. The other members of Stalker Force didn't bother to look back as they ran.

Nguyen sprinted after them, pumping his arms, whimpering and simultaneously suffocating through the frigid monsoon. He took a chance to look over his shoulder and saw Scarecrow and Mr. Crowley chasing after him, struggling with Dutch's contorted body between them. The Father T. rex was gaining speed, easily cutting through the three-foot deep mud with each splashing step. The tyrannosaur lowered its head and spread its toothy jaws for Dutch to scream into.

"*Fuck it,*" Scarecrow barked. "Less one, Mr. Crowley!"

Scarecrow and Mr. Crowley let go of Dutch, dropping him onto his back in the mud. Dutch continued to scream until the Father T. rex lunged forward and snapped its jaws over his abdomen, splitting him in half. The only thing keeping Dutch together as the tyrannosaur lifted him were its tightly clamped jaws. Dutch continued to flail and scream until the Father T. rex dropped him from twenty feet in the air. As soon as the jaws parted, Dutch's body separated and tumbled to the ground from either side of the Father T. rex's head.

Scarecrow and Mr. Crowley had barely made it more than ten feet without Dutch before the Father T. rex redirected its attention to them. The Father T. rex ripped its fangs through the entrails that still connected Dutch's corpse with a twist of its head. The tyrannosaur roared at Scarecrow and Mr. Crowley, his eyes alight like fire, seething with ravenous fury.

[46]

Nguyen stared in shock. He couldn't comprehend Scarecrow's actions.

"Run, dink!" Scarecrow barked, shoving Nguyen aside. Nguyen blinked a few times, saw Mr. Crowley sprint past, and turned to see the Father T. rex barreling towards him, howling through parting jaws. Nguyen's nervous system electrocuted his core and he sprang to life, charging after Scarecrow and Stalker Force into the twisted confines of the jungle.

The Father T. rex chased them all the way to the helicopter.

Stalker Force and the Hyenas clambered through the undergrowth, squeezing their bodies through nets of vines, slashing machetes and daggers through the banana leaves and rhododendron that filled every inch of space from the forest floor to the understory canopy. The Father T. rex pursued them relentlessly with the focus and fury of a vengeful parent. The behemoth gnawed through the undergrowth, snapped his jaws through the saplings, and crushed everything in his path underfoot.

Xavier and Stalker Force were working their way up to the peak of a hill. Nguyen and Scarecrow were at the back of the group, heaving themselves through the wiry branches of rhododendron. Scarecrow raised his head and saw the moonlight filtering through the clouds above, cutting through the tree-line at the top of the hill. The helicopter's bubbled cockpit window gleamed like obsidian as it caught the nocturnal rays.

"We're here," Scarecrow shouted, aiming a trembling arm at the craft concealed beyond the edge of the forest. "There it is!"

The Father T. rex bellowed in response and the men climbed harder, fighting more viciously for every inch between them and the helicopter. Xavier and

[47]

Stalker Force were out first, with Andrei running to the cockpit to get the pilot ready for an immediate take-off. The rotor blades began to thump and wind slashed through the undergrowth, washing over the dampened bodies of the men. Mr. Crowley was out of the forest next, practically leaping into the cabin.

Nguyen dug his fingers through the vegetation and dragged himself higher. He kicked for purchase only to get further tangled in the foliage. He panted as he swung his machete around his legs, cleaving the clawing hands of the undergrowth. Scarecrow's head emerged through the taro leaves and Nguyen reached a hand to him. When he looked past Scarecrow's frantic eyes, he saw the Father T. rex's snout rising above the undergrowth behind him.

The Father T. rex was huffing with effort, forced to crawl through the thick bodies of elder durian trees that couldn't be moved. The tyrannosaur's eyes locked onto the back of Scarecrow's head.

Nguyen saw the Father T. rex's jaws widening, the black pit of its throat visible through rows of serrated teeth. Nguyen felt a hand around his ankle and he swung his machete without thinking, simply screaming and reacting.

The machete met no resistance as it severed Scarecrow's hand.

Nguyen stared in shock, uncomprehending and unfeeling. His spirit was swimming through his body as he stared at Scarecrow's pinched eyes. Scarecrow was screaming, clutching at the bloody stump of his forearm, still crawling towards Nguyen. The Father T. rex dragged itself closer, writhing through the vegetation like an immense snake, kicking back with its legs to propel its snapping jaws closer.

Nguyen gripped the machete.

[48]

Scarecrow reached for Nguyen, but he was met by the swinging blade. The machete chopped half-way through Shadow's shoulder, splashing blood across Nguyen's face. Scarecrow continued to scream, with more bloodlust than pain, and Nguyen continued to hack and swing the machete until there were no more screams to be heard.

The Father T. rex heaved itself forward and snapped its jaws around Scarecrow's limp, mutilated carcass. Nguyen stared, wide-eyed and drenched in steaming blood, the machete forgotten in his hands.

Nguyen was no longer inhibited by the jungle. It seemed as if the forest had relinquished its grip on his body, and he quickly slithered through the undergrowth and into the open air of the hill-top. The rest of the men were already inside of the helicopter, shouting for him to hurry, waving him on. Nguyen looked back and saw the Father T. rex's quill-covered snout forcing itself through the tree-line.

Nguyen sheathed the machete without thinking. When he hopped into the helicopter, he was deaf to the questions the other men were shouting. *Why are you covered in blood? Where's Scarecrow? Why aren't you saying anything?*

Nguyen felt nothing; said nothing.

The helicopter lifted off of the hill, bucking in the wind and the rain. Nguyen ignored the conversations and arguments between Stalker Force. He wiped the blood from his face with his trembling hands. The screams of Dutch and Scarecrow were fresh and perpetual in Nguyen's mind. The Father T. rex roared at the helicopter from the hill top, but Nguyen was deaf and indifferent to the ravenous carnivore.

Mr. Crowley never took his eyes off of Nguyen.

[49]

MR. CROWLEY

Xavier was unable to sleep following the deaths of Dutch and Scarecrow.

It wasn't the horrific nature of the deaths that had fueled Xavier's insomnia; it was the trap set by Sobek, the mysterious alpha utahraptor with a crown of kaprosuchus tusks, that had kept Xavier wide-eyed and anxious through the night. While the rest of Stalker Force dozed heavily in their bunks, Xavier had tossed and turned with the tumultuous possibilities that Sobek's trap had presented. Xavier and Andrei had always known the utahraptors to be exceedingly cunning, but neither could have ever predicted that they would be tricked into walking up to a tyrannosaurus nest.

Xavier couldn't deny the dangers that the truth presented.

At 0600, Xavier finally gave up on the idea of beating his insomnia and left his bunk. The monsoon hadn't let up from the night before; as soon as Xavier stepped out of the cabin, he was met by the roar of rain crashing upon the sheet-metal awning. Xavier sat in a metal folding chair, put his boots up on the porch railing, and started sharpening his machete with a pocket whetstone. He sat there in silence for a while, slowly drawing the stone along the length of the blade in a steady rhythm until the entire previous night and its implications had been washed from his mind.

Xavier allowed the pattering rainfall to cleanse his consciousness.

After a stretch of time without measure, Xavier's trance was broken by the creaking of the cabin door's hinges. Xavier didn't bother to turn when he heard

[50]

Andrei shuffle outside. Xavier grunted a brief 'hello' and Andrei sat down in a folding chair beside him. Xavier took a canteen from his web belt and handed it to Andrei.

Andrei took the canteen and sniffed; day-old C-ration coffee.

"Mmf," Andrei took a swig, grimaced, and handed it back to Xavier. "You can keep that."

"Suit yourself," Xavier shrugged. He took a long pull from the canteen and exhaled a noxious whirlwind of stale coffee breath. "What are you doing up this early? Nightmares about the Cyclops again?"

"No," Andrei said. He shuddered; Xavier couldn't tell if it was the chill in the air or the mention of the Cyclops that had triggered it. "I was up all night thinking about what happened. Nguyen and those masked men. The black ops team or whatever Jericho calls them."

"MACV-SOG," Xavier said. "Or, at least that's what Jericho says they are. Then again, he really seems keen on that 'Hyenas' nickname. For all we know, they could be para-military mercenaries. It's not like we can send our concerns anywhere up the wire. This war is all loose ends, nothing substantial other than body counts..."

The whetstone rasped as Xavier's shaking fist slipped across the blade.

"...And I'm sure all of those masked men have higher body counts than any of us could ever think to fathom."

"And now Nguyen's a part of it," Andrei said with a sad shake of his head. "Poor kid. Poor, stupid, stupid fucking kid."

"Hey now," Xavier said, tapping Andrei's shoulder with the tip of the machete. "You're just as wrapped up in Jericho's shit now as Nguyen is. Same as me, it seems. You catch what the Hyenas were even doing at the Ash-Tray? Looked like they were trying to find some intel. Any idea what that intel might have been?"

Andrei remained silent for a minute, staring off to the mist-veiled tree-line at the edge of the electric perimeter fence. He was rubbing the goosebumps from his bare arms to no avail. Each list of the wind carried a thousand licks from Vietnam's dank tongue. Andrei shivered, closing his eyes.

"Borodin's office," Andrei said. "They could have been after anything. Coordinates to nearby Russian, NVA, or Viet Cong settlements. Maybe to see if they had any catalogued information on the dinosaurs that we haven't thought of. There's also the likeliest possibility; the one I don't want to think about."

"The Collider," Xavier muttered.

"Right," Andrei sighed, opening his eyes. "I tried to warn Ryan that this would happen. There's no way we can redirect General Jericho from whatever crash course he's got us on. There are plenty of reasons for him to be interested in this valley, but it's clearly not the dinosaurs."

"Power," Xavier said, nodding solemnly. "Continuing an arms race."

Andrei extended a cupped hand beyond the protection of the awning, allowing his palm to fill with fat, frigid rain drops.

"We're on the same page," Andrei mumbled. "I knew we would be. I'm practically a prisoner to Jericho; he's never mentioned sending me to the United States, letting me go, nothing. I think I may have sold my soul to study these

[52]

dinosaurs. The moment Ryan brought me onto Vulture Squad's mission, I was as good as Jericho's."

Xavier briefly tensed at the mention of his former Captain's name. He slowly sheathed his machete with a trembling hand. He clenched and unclenched his fist sporadically, casting his eyes back to the fog that hung over the muddy clearing. Andrei cleared his throat awkwardly.

"Sorry," Andrei coughed.

Xavier shook his head briefly. He laughed a little, but his eyes remained as wide and vacant as burned-out light-bulbs.

"Fresh wounds," Xavier mumbled. "That's all."

"So what are we going to do?" Andrei asked. "You know, about Jericho. Should we go demand him for information? Ask him about Nguyen and the Hyenas, what they were looking for?"

Xavier shook his head again, this time deliberately.

"We're going to keep doing our job," Xavier said. "We have no leverage, Andrei. We aren't going after another collider now; we're hunting and quarantining dinosaurs. Just about anybody could do this job at this point; I'm sure the SEALS would kill for the opportunity. Or Delta Force."

"They could also bomb the entire valley," Andrei shrugged. "Yet they haven't, for some reason. Why do you think that is?"

"It's a good cover," Xavier said. "Jericho likes his deniability."

[53]

Andrei was mulling over Xavier's sentiments when there was the sharp *bang* of a thrown-open door bouncing off of a wall. Mr. Crowley, the only surviving Hyena other than Nguyen, came storming out of Jericho's office. The lithe black-uniformed agent kicked through the mud, spitting and swearing on his path towards the barracks. Andrei started to get up, but Xavier waved him down.

"I've got it," Xavier said. He rose to his feet and cupped his hands around his mouth, shouting over the rain. "Can I help you?"

Mr. Crowley didn't answer. In a matter of seconds he was close enough for Xavier to see his emerald eyes burning hot from within the small opening of the black balaclava. It gave Xavier a moment of déjà vu, of facing his former captain after liberating so many Viet Cong internment camps. Xavier suddenly felt his throat tighten, his Adam's apple constricting into a suffocating knot.

"*Sir-*"

"Get the fuck out of my way," Mr. Crowley grunted, shouldering past Xavier. Andrei rose to his feet, but Mr. Crowley shoved him off of the porch and into the mud with a single thrust of his arm.

Xavier grabbed Mr. Crowley's extended arm and threw him against the barrack's wall. Mr. Crowley quickly planted his foot against the wall, halting his momentum, and immediately pivoted back towards Xavier. Before Xavier could react, Mr. Crowley had withdrawn his own machete and had it poised between Xavier's eyes. Both Xavier and Andrei went still.

"*Where's the gook*," Mr. Crowley growled.

"What-"

"The *gook*," Mr. Crowley repeated, sheathing the machete. His eyes were wild with hate, manic and strained from a sleepless night. "*Nguyen. Panther.* Where is he?"

"Sleeping," Xavier said. "He passed out in our barracks last night while talking to me and Andrei. Why?"

Mr. Crowley turned from Xavier and threw open the door to the barracks. Xavier and Andrei followed him inside, where the rain took on the effect of muted percussion. Mr. Crowley went from bunk to bunk, glancing at the sleeping men of Stalker Force, until he set his eyes on Nguyen's young, bronzed face. Mr. Crowley immediately took hold of Nguyen's shoulders and wrenched him from his cot.

Nguyen awoke screaming, swinging his arms frantically without thinking. He grabbed onto Mr. Crowley's throat with one hand and withdrew his machete with the other. Xavier and Andrei began shouting, trying to get Mr. Crowley off of Nguyen. The other members of Stalker Force began to rouse from their sleep, muttering things like 'the hell,' and 'c'mon man,' as Nguyen shouted and swung his blade.

Mr. Crowley shouldered aside Xavier and Andrei as he dragged Nguyen out of the barracks, beyond the shelter of the awning, and threw him face-down in the mud. Nguyen scrambled through the foot-deep soil, slippery and red like the blood drained from a pig.

Mr. Crowley kicked the machete from Nguyen's hand. His boot snapped the bones in Nguyen's fingers, twisting and contorting them to a mixture of acute and obtuse angles. Nguyen howled as Mr. Crowley grabbed him by the throat and raised him off his feet, holding him high up into the low-lying clouds. Xavier and Andrei ran to the awning. Andrei was about to run out into the storm but Xavier kept him back.

"Don't," Xavier whispered to Andrei. "Just listen."

"*Scarecrow*," Mr. Crowley stated coldly.

Nguyen dug his fingers into Mr. Crowley's wrists. He couldn't breathe; the grey light filtering through the clouds turned dim in Nguyen's eyes. Mr. Crowley shook Nguyen forcefully, but his grip was turning weak.

"*Answer me*," Mr. Crowley thundered. "*Scarecrow*."

"That's…not…" Nguyen wheezed. "…not…a question…"

Mr. Crowley threw Nguyen into the mud at his feet. He threw a boot into Nguyen's gut, folding the young native in half. Mr. Crowley pulled off his balaclava as he paced around Nguyen.

The skin of Mr. Crowley's face was pale to the point of near-translucence. Steel-wool muttonchops framed his scarred, narrow face. Vengeful fury swam through his glimmering green eyes as he knelt down to stare into Nguyen's pupils.

"You were with him," Mr. Crowley seethed through cigarette-stained teeth. "You were covered in his blood. Why didn't you help him? Why didn't you bring back the body of your captain?"

"The – the rex – " Nguyen gasped. "- ate him, I couldn't-"

[56]

Mr. Crowley smacked Nguyen across the face, twisting his neck with the force of the strike.

"Again," Mr. Crowley said. "Tell me why you didn't bring your Captain's body back. Why didn't you get him out of there? Why didn't you fire your rifle!?"

"I didn't-didn't," Nguyen stammered, shielding his face, curling into a fetal position. Mr. Crowley continued to circle him, kicking at his back, legs, stomach and neck, constantly prodding and pounding with the tip of his boot.

"*Talk,*" Mr. Crowley hissed. "Talk, fucking *dink. Talk!*"

"*I couldn't stop,*" Nguyen cried, wrapping his arms around his head. "*I just-just-*"

"*Sobbing*; fucking child," Mr. Crowley spat. "I told Jericho to kill you. Fucking Viet Cong *traitor*. You're just another Charlie *gook* behind the wire. I killed so many like you sneaking into our bases, acting like people, acting like *us*. I want you *dead*, gook, fucking *dead*."

Xavier started to walk through the rain towards Mr. Crowley and Nguyen. Molnar, the CQB specialist of Stalker Force, was striding up behind him.

"That's enough," Xavier barked through the wind. "Leave him alone, grunt. I can already tell you that this kid is more important to Jericho than you could ever be. Jericho catch's wind of this, your ass will be back on a plane in a leather body bag."

[57]

"Or buried outside the perimeter," Molnar said, twitching his head towards the tree-line. "We can even make it look like a utahraptor killed ya, if you prefer."

"This *gook* got my captain killed," Mr. Crowley snapped, jabbing his finger at Nguyen as he looked from Molnar to Xavier. "I'm not working in any outfit with this double-crossing Charlie *fuck*. He's VC; we all know it."

Nguyen suddenly grabbed Mr. Crowley's boots and yanked his feet out from under him. Mr. Crowley hit the ground on his back, his head ricocheting off the bottom of a soupy puddle. Nguyen climbed on top of his stunned team-mate and started pounding his good fist into Mr. Crowley's eye sockets. Mr. Crowley barked obscenities as Xavier and Molnar dragged Nguyen off.

"*I'm not VC*," Nguyen screamed. "*Tôi sẽ giết bạn!*"

"*Nguyen*," Andrei said, raising his eyebrows.

Mr. Crowley jumped to his feet and started back-pedaling away from the others. He was wide-eyed with a sudden fear that came with the flow of blood from between his swollen, blackened lids. He pointed a shaking finger at Nguyen as he turned back to Jericho's office.

"I'll remember this," Mr. Crowley said, glancing at Xavier and Andrei. "I won't forget this shit, I'll have you all trussed like pigs in the trees if I see any of you near me. I sleep with one eye open, *Panther. Remember that.* Touch me and I'll kill you. *I promise-*"

"CROWLEY!"

[58]

General Jericho was standing in the doorway of his office. He was a shadow caught within the scant lamp-light that ebbed from the cabin. Mr. Crowley cast one last caustic look to Stalker Force before returning to his beckoning master. Xavier helped Nguyen to his feet as Jericho's door slammed shut. Molnar dusted the mud from Nguyen's filthy uniform.

"You'll be okay?" Xavier asked.

Nguyen glanced into Xavier's eyes, and the wordless information communicated between their gaze was enough to fill Xavier with a chill that trumped the cascading rainfall. Xavier felt himself go numb from within.

Nguyen quickly turned and bolted across the clearing to the infirmary, throwing the door shut behind him. Xavier, Andrei, and Molnar stood in the rain, soaked and confused.

"Andrei, did you catch what Nguyen said?" Xavier asked.

"That Vietnamese bit at the end?" Andrei asked, rubbing his throat.

Xavier nodded.

"*I'll kill you*," Andrei said. "That's what he said."

"I think he meant it," Xavier mumbled gravely.

"I wouldn't blame him," Andrei sighed, wiping his glasses off on his sleeve. "That sadist has a serious stick up his ass."

"No time to worry about any of that drama," Xavier said. "We should get to the war-room. We need to talk about the Quetzalcoatlus."

[59]

AGONY

The sky was veined with amber and ember-red light as the sun dissolved behind the valley walls. A lone black shape, like a dragonfly darting through the clouds, slowly circled the patchwork of floodplains that were stitched together by the river's tributaries. Xavier Wise and Stalker Force had been summoned to slaughter the valley's deadliest aerial inhabitants; a pair of Quetzalcoatlus that reigned supreme over the territory previously abandoned by their kin.

A freshly butchered water buffalo had been strung like an ornament from the landing skids of Stalker Force's helicopter. Scarlet mist frothed from the lacerated stump of the buffalo's neck. The plan was to use the be-headed buffalo as bait for the Quetzalcoatlus. Only two quetzalcoatlus had remained after Vulture Squad's initial foray into the valley, and it was Stalker Force's immediate objective to eliminate the pair of aerial predators before they could migrate.

"The blood should draw the Quetzalcoatlus out from hiding," Andrei Wynn called back from the cockpit. "Once they pick up the scent and tail us, we have to put them out of the sky. Try to only kill one if you can; we need to back-track the other in case they share a nest."

"Dripping blood from a buffalo," Molnar said, shaking his head. "I wish I was a part of that conversation."

"Do we need to worry about any other animals?" Konnor asked. "I imagine leaving a trail of blood might make some other predators take notice, right boss?"

"Right," Xavier said, nodding. "That's why we're not landing anywhere except for Jericho's base until we get these birds out of the air. We don't want to set the helicopter down and ring a dinner bell for the utahraptors and kaprosuchus…"

[60]

"So has anybody, uh…" Molnar twirled a hand in the air, trying to find the right words. "Has anybody…looked up the dinosaurs' skirts, or something? What if there's no nest at all and we just end up wasting time looking for it?"

"We can't risk it," Andrei shouted, craning his head into the cabin through the cockpit. "If a single Quetzalcoatlus leaves this valley alive it could have untold consequences. We have to assume that every Quetzalcoatlus is a pregnant female ready to populate another country out of our reach."

"Unless there were more than the original three, and they already left," Konnor said with a shrug. "Dr. Wynn, you were alone for what, a year? There could have been dozens of these things flying around the place. They could have already migrated by the time Vulture Squad got here. You think about that?"

"Believe me, I have," Andrei muttered, turning forward in his seat. "Better hope that hypothesis doesn't get tested."

Andrei peered through the phosphorescent-flaring clouds. The light of the setting sun made it difficult for him to see through the golden cotton masses. The pilot beside him cursed beneath his breath, a hand shielding his eyes as the helicopter descended.

When the helicopter fell through the bottom of the clouds the men inside were rewarded with a glimpse of the valley in its sun-soaked splendor. Tawny light reflected from the surface of every rock, tree, and stream. The river itself was blindingly bright, a thick line of shining crystalline fractals coiling and weaving through the basin. Andrei had to take a pair of Ray-Bans from his breast pocket and snap them over his glasses to keep from being blinded.

"See anything?" Xavier asked, craning his head into the cockpit.

[61]

"Lots of sun spots," Andrei grumbled. "No pterosaurs."

"*Syd*," Xavier barked, turning back into the cabin. "Get on the gun."

"Roger that," Syd said.

Syd rose from his seat, teetering as the helicopter swayed in the wind. There was an M-47 minigun mounted to the doorway of the cabin. Syd pulled open the cabin door, allowing the gusts of wind to blow through the interior of the helicopter. The rotor blades were deafening, but the wind consumed all else. Syd growled irritably as he clambered into the gunner seat mounted to the door-frame. The M-47 was connected just below the seat so that the user could swing their legs around either side of the stock.

Syd grinned as he settled into the well-worn leather padded seat. It had been months since he had last mounted a helicopter's gunner seat. Normally he had aimed the miniguns in the direction of rice paddy farmers, back when he had served with Tiger Force, but there were no other humans in the valley for miles around. If anything happened to the helicopter, their only hope of escape would be a call for reinforcements from further south; Jericho's base.

A million possibilities lie within the time it would take for an evac to arrive.

The wind tugged at Syd's cheeks as he directed the minigun towards the bow of the helicopter. His facial features were stretched back as the gusts dragged against his skin. Snot billowed through his wind-whipped handle-bar moustache. He was feeling pretty good from his position on high; it brought him back to his time flying down freeways on motorcycles with the likes of the Hell's Angels and the Gypsys.

Syd glanced into the cabin and caught Molnar pointing at him, guffawing.

[62]

"*What*," Syd barked, barely audible beneath the swinging rotor blades.

"Looking good, Hunter S.," Molnar hollered back.

Syd scowled. He knew of some authors, but not a lot. He had spent most of his time studying poets, not gonzo-journalists. He continued pondering whom this 'Hunter S' could be, or what kind of beatnik jargon it might mean. Molnar was a sheet-freak from the streets of San Francisco, after all. How the degenerate drug abuser could have climbed his way into the special forces was beyond Syd's realm of understanding.

Molnar was still shouting at Syd. It was difficult for Syd to understand his words, but he was able to draw an answer from reading his lips.

Check the cow.

Syd glanced down, tilting away from the mini-gun to properly see below the helicopter. He had a brief flare of anxiety when he spotted the upper canopy a hundred feet below like moss beneath a magnifying glass. There wasn't a seat-belt; he hoped to god that if anything happened, he wouldn't go flying out. He had heard Xavier's story about Miller and Nguyen. The last thing Syd wanted was to free-fall into the realm of monsters.

The nylon tethers that were strung from the helicopter's undercarriage were fluttering in the breeze. Syd narrowed his eyes as he followed the length of nylon to the halves of the buffalo bouncing and dropping innards in the wind. Syd rubbed his jaw and tightened a hand around the grip of the minigun as the bloody hunks of flesh performed a macabre dance mid-air.

"Hey boss," Syd shouted, craning his neck back. "Was the buffalo in one piece when we took off?"

[63]

"*What?*" Xavier cried back.

"*I said,*" Syd thundered, "*Was the buffalo in one piece?*"

"*What?*"

"*He said,*" Molnar interjected. "Was the buffalo in one piece?"

Syd rolled his eyes and looked below. While Xavier and Molnar shouted at Syd, he focused on the lengths of nylon and their butchered ornaments. One of the halves of the buffalo was missing; the other was still tied up in its tethers. He assumed that one of the halves had fallen out of its binds, lost to the forest floor below. Perhaps some deinonychus would enjoy the easy meal, or the Father T. rex would eat the remains in one mouthful. It was impossible to tell.

Syd was still staring at the remaining buffalo halve when a silhouette formed within the clouds behind the helicopter. The silhouette was a solid black figure sifting through the golden-blazing veil; it was as easy to make out as a fish in an aquarium tank. The details of the animal's body sharpened as it flew towards the helicopter. First the beak broke through the clouds, spearing into the open air like a shark fin cresting fog-laden waves.

"*Quetzalcoatlus,*" Syd screamed.

The helicopter rapidly ascended at an acute angle, rising higher in the sky. Syd felt gravity pull his ass lower into the seat, and he instinctively wrapped his thick arms around the minigun for stability. The helicopter tilted to the left, turning away as the quetzalcoatlus breezed past the undercarriage. Syd tugged his legs up as the quetzalcoatlus's beak whistled past his boots.

Syd's jaw fell open; the quetzalcoatlus was as big as a fighter jet.

Leathery skin draped in pubic-like protofeathers swept beneath Syd's feet. The Quetzalcoatlus glanced at Syd from over its shoulder as the helicopter tilted away from the animal. Syd was so shocked that he was incapable of pulling the trigger. There were no thoughts within his mind; mere awe was all that he was capable of in the face of such an immense air-borne animal.

The nylon tethers from the landing skids were ensnared in its beak.

"*Shoot 'er*," Xavier screamed. "*Shoot her!*"

Syd pulled the trigger too late.

The tether snapped taut in the quetzalcoatlus's jaws and the helicopter bucked backwards from the sudden brake. The helicopter began to spin wildly in the air, set off-balance by the violent shift in inertia. Syd screamed as he was swung around in the open air like an astronaut in centrifuge training. The mini-gun caterwauled as it fired from between his legs, bullets churning through the air as the helicopter spun round and round. Syd heard the quetzalcoatlus honk in pain, and the tether was released.

The helicopter evened-out and settled into a hover. The craft's landing skid had been bent by the force of the quetzalcoatlus, but otherwise, no other damage had been done to the helicopter. When Syd finally managed to pull his eyes up from the canopy below, he caught sight of the quetzalcoatlus half-listing through the air. The stretched membrane that consisted of half the animal's wing-span had been turned to swiss by the minigun. The quetzalcoatlus howled as it fell helplessly to the floodplains beyond the canopy.

Syd watched the tumbling quetzalcoatlus until it finally crashed into the earth. He kept his finger on the trigger of the M47, but didn't pull it. He saw some rogue male kaprosuchus lurking in the floodplain and wanted to see what would happen when they found the fallen pterosaur.

"Oh my," Molnar said, leering over Syd's shoulder. "He didn't quite stick the landing."

"Fuck off," Syd grunted. He pulled the trigger and emptied several dozen rounds into the backside of the dying quetzalcoatlus. The pterosaur's torso was ripped apart, leaving only a pureed mess for the kaprosuchus to consume. Molnar groaned in disgust as he hunkered back down in his seat within the cabin.

"Weak," Molnar said, shaking his head. "Could have had a show."

"Something to write home about?" Syd asked.

"Something to tell my therapist," Molnar mumbled.

"Where's the other bird?" Xavier called out.

"No idea," Syd barked. He swung the mini-gun around, but he didn't see any other aberrant shapes in the sky. The helicopter lazily swept around the floodplain, providing the men inside with a full view of the slain quetzalcoatlus being consumed by several rogue male kaprosuchus. Syd stared silently as one of the kaprosuchus sheared through the dead quetzalcoatlus's fresh-ground torso with its dagger-length fangs.

An unfamiliar shadow slid over the armored backs of the feasting kaprosuchus. The kaprosuchus turned their snouts to the sky and started barking, stamping their feet and braying like angered grizzly bears. Syd looked up as well and saw a great black winged beast barreling down through the clouds, towards the floodplain.

[66]

An agonized baritone howl announced the arrival of the second quetzalcoatlus. The pterosaur folded its wings and dropped down onto all fours across the clearing from the kaprosuchus rogues. The quetzalcoatlus's beady eyes were alight with horror and anger; emotions that had never been divined from the stoic creatures.

The kaprosuchus weren't afraid of the towering pterosaur; each of the crocodilian creatures were at the height of physical maturity. The rogue kaprosuchus were much larger and more robust than their younger brethren that trawled the waterways. The largest kaprosuchus, as heavily built and muscular as a polar bear, lunged over the dead quetzalcoatlus to claim the kill for itself. The other males directed their attention at the approaching quetzalcoatlus, attempting to fend it off by barking and snapping their tusk-framed jaws.

The surviving Quetzalcoatlus wasn't amused.

"Wait," Andrei shouted to the others onboard. "Hold your fire."

One of the kaprosuchus lunged at the quetzalcoatlus, but the pterosaur easily leapt into the air and beat its wings, ascending above the crocodilian predator. Just as the kaprosuchus splashed down into the marsh, the quetzalcoatlus dropped down on top of it. The quetzalcoatlus covered the smaller carnivore as it punched its beak in and out of the kaprosuchus's spine. The kaprosuchus immediately collapsed and spasmed in the ankle-deep water as the quetzalcoatlus withdrew its bloodied beak.

The kaprosuchus rogues weren't easily deterred.

The surviving kaprosuchus charged the Quetzalcoatlus in an attempt to dog-pile the larger predator. The quetzalcoatlus feigned away from one kaprosuchus and swung its beak along the crocodilomorph's exposed belly. The razor-tipped keratin sheath on the quetzalcoatlus's beak sliced through the kaprosuchus's underbelly, creating a laceration that vivisected the animal. The kaprosuchus howled as its organs spilled from its tumbling body.

"Holy *shit*," Molnar exclaimed.

The four remaining kaprosuchus circled the quetzalcoatlus. The quetzalcoatlus was trapped; it couldn't outrun the kaprosuchus on foot, and the carnivores were too close for it to take flight. Syd found himself tightening his grip around the mini-gun. He had to fight the urge to fire upon the kaprosuchus; he couldn't risk killing the quetzalcoatlus without first finding its nest.

Syd knew the quetzalcoatlus could handle the kaprosuchus itself.

The largest kaprosuchus charged first, galloping across the floodplain towards the quetzalcoatlus. The other three kaprosuchus lunged for the quetzalcoatlus's back. The quetzalcoatlus turned around and jammed its beak through the widening jaws of an air-borne kaprosuchus. The keratin-tipped beak punched a hole straight through the back of the kaprosuchus's skull. The other two kaprosuchus collided with the freshly-speared carcass and went sprawling to the ground. The crocodilians raked their claws at one another as they fought to climb out of their dog-pile.

While the kaprosuchus were snapping at one another, the Quetzalcoatlus studied his victims. The pterosaur's eyes worked like those of a mortician analyzing a body prepped for autopsy. It caught weaknesses in the bodies of the kaprosuchus and attacked accordingly. The quetzalcoatlus lunged for the largest kaprosuchus first, which was distracted by a lesser kaprosuchus nipping at his legs.

[68]

The quetzalcoatlus's tongue shot forth from its opened beak and wrapped around the throat of the largest kaprosuchus. The ensnared carnivore attempted to claw at the barbed appendage slithering around his neck, but couldn't reach. The other two kaprosuchus snorted and barked as they backed away from the quetzalcoatlus. The smaller carnivores were shocked as they watched the quetzalcoatlus spread its wings, rising on its hind legs to its full height.

The ensnared kaprosuchus rose on its hind-legs as it was lynched.

The quetzalcoatlus manipulated the kaprosuchus like a rangler tussling with a rodeo bull. It paced around the kaprosuchus so the strangled carnivore couldn't turn around to attack, while simultaneously tugging its tongue back further and further up into its beak. The kaprosuchus could only gasp for air and grunt breathlessly as its throat was pinched shut.

The quetzalcoatlus's tongue suddenly relinquished the kaprosuchus and the burly crocodilian belly-flopped to the ground. Before the kaprosuchus could even move, the quetzalcoatlus brought its head down like an axe and pierced its beak through the kaprosuchus's cranium. The kaprosuchus's legs trembled with the last impulses of its nervous system before finally turning rigid.

The quetzalcoatlus turned its beak to the two remaining kaprosuchus.

The kaprosuchus looked at one another, then back to the dead alpha.

Without another sound, the kaprosuchus turned and bolted across the clearing, trotting like wolves to their perspective corners of the flood-plain. The quetzalcoatlus honked at the rogues as they fled, spreading its wings in a display of territorial dominance. The men of Stalker Force fell silent as they listened to the furious vocalizations of the last surviving quetzalcoatlus in the valley.

[69]

"Mother of God," Konnor mumbled.

"In'nit just?" Molnar said.

"Syd, open fire," Xavier said. "We gotta chase it home."

Syd almost felt a pang of remorse as he aimed the mini-gun between the quetzalcoatlus's legs. He normally felt nothing when it came to taking the lives of others, especially animals; the rest of the team was still ignorant of Syd's farm-animal slaughtering repertoire with Tiger Force. Many domesticated animals had fallen beneath his swinging machete, dooming Vietnamese villages to starvation.

There were a lot of things nobody knew about Syd.

"*Open fire*," Xavier barked.

Syd allowed the barrel of the minigun to drop between the Quetzalcoatlus's legs. What little empathy that remained in Syd's brutish shell had begun to resonate with the quetzalcoatlus. He could relate to the pterosaur's ferocity and the precision with which it cut down the kaprosuchus that threatened to destroy its mate's corpse. The slaughter that Syd had dealt to the innocent of Vietnam had been done in the name of redemption, in avenging those slaughtered American draftee's that he often found pierced by punji stakes or butchered by machetes.

The animal only wanted to mourn its ally; perhaps Syd was anthropomorphizing the quetzalcoatlus, but his own heart was one of animalistic brutality and vengeance. Syd had been in similar positions before, but he had dealt the blows to the Viet Cong by hand. The Viet Cong that he captured were butchered by blade, not by rifle; the return on their murderous investment had to be returned with an eye for an eye of suffering.

[70]

Syd pulled the trigger.

The quetzalcoatlus took flight, soaring high above the canopy. The lone pterosaur looked over its shoulder and honked as the helicopter gave chase. Syd narrowed his eyes as the wind clawed at his tear ducts. As the quetzalcoatlus flew to the highest mountain peaks that penned in the valley, Syd sifted through unfamiliar and long-buried emotions.

Syd knew that he had to be the one to kill the quetzalcoatlus.

Only a true killer deserved to kill another.

AGONY II

Starlight needled through the black sheet of the midnight-indigo sky, embroidering the constellations into a twinkling tapestry. The helicopter carrying Stalker Force hummed and bounced around the burly shoulders of a cragged mountain peak like an inquisitive botfly. Xavier Wise was in the cockpit, leaning over Andrei's shoulder to look through the bullet-scratched windshield. Xavier and Andrei were muttering to one another through the cacophonous rotor blades. Andrei pointed out a sunken cave mouth yawning from a ledge littered with palm fronds, ferns, and thorny shrubs.

"There he is," Andrei said. "The last quetzalcoatlus."

The widower quetzalcoatlus was climbing into the cave on all fours like a bat returning to its hovel. The immense pterosaur clung to the crumbling rock wall with its clawed feet and fore-fingers, kicking sand and loose slabs of stone down the mountainside as it crawled. Xavier and Andrei watched as the quetzalcoatlus ducked into the cave mouth and instantly fell into the dark depths within. Andrei imagined himself being swallowed whole within the mountain and shuddered.

"Looks like we're here," Andrei said. "Based on how that quetzalcoatlus just…vanished…I think it's safe to assume it's a straight drop inside. Do we have any flamethrowers? Something to flush it out or maybe burn the cave from the inside-out?"

"Flamethrower's out," Xavier said. "Molnar wasted the fuel during the bonfire the other night."

"It's cruel to burn things alive," Molnar shouted from the cabin.

"No shit," Xavier grunted. "But that doesn't mean waste all of the fuel trying to torch some dead palm trees!"

"Better to blaze trees than to flambé birds," Molnar said. "Unless we eat 'em afterwards. Test out that 'everything tastes like chicken' theory."

Andrei rolled his eyes.

"Everybody, get ready to rappel down," Xavier said, moving from the cockpit to the cabin. "Molnar, don't forget to leave your harness behind."

"What harness?" Molnar said. "All I've got is my helmet."

"Too late for a helmet to do anything," Konnor muttered. "Brain's already scrambled. What's another hit to the head gonna do?"

The men of Stalker Force rappelled from the helicopter to a lower ledge on the cliff-face. The climb was easy enough, despite the loose rocks and slate shifting beneath their feet. Xavier led the way with Syd Kinane and Andrei Wynn by his side. When they stepped up to the landing of the cave, the pebbles kicked by their boots went skipping into the dank mouth and down hundreds of feet through empty air. The only sign of the pebbles hitting the floor were the delicate *clicks* that followed several seconds later.

Xavier craned his head into the chamber and whistled.

"Fantastic."

The recess of the cave entrance only went back several feet; the floor, however, was nearly a hundred feet below. From what Xavier could gleam from the

[73]

moonlight reflected within, the cave itself was the length of a football field, complete with stalagmites that mirrored a bed of chiseled-stone nails. The open air of the cavern was thick with a dewy fog that blurred and distorted the shapes of the rock formations below. The only way into the forest of stalagmites was to jump.

"Our bird's somewhere down there," Xavier said. "Everybody, get your rappelling gear out. We're dropping in."

The men of Stalker Force fastened their anchors to the thick stump of a Dalat pine and snapped into their harnesses. Andrei was without rappelling equipment or any expertise in the practice, so he was forced to cling to Molnar's back as they back-pedaled to the entrance of the cave. Molnar leapt back into the cave, practically free-falling to the jagged stalagmites below as Andrei howled from his back.

Molnar gave the rope belay a tight squeeze and quickly halted their rapid descent. The pair swung back towards the cave wall, and Molnar gracefully planted his boots against the granite. Andrei looked back and forth as Xavier and Konnor descended beside him. Andrei shook his head wildly when Molnar coiled his legs to kick off from the wall.

"C'mon," Andrei whined. "Slow down-"

"Ain't no brakes with a damaged brain," Molnar said, grinning wide.

Molnar kicked off of the rock wall and descended another fifteen feet down the rope with Andrei on his back. Molnar continued sliding down the rope at an increasingly rapid pace, spacing his jumps so that they would slide down ten feet, then fifteen, twenty, until they was nearly sliding down a quarter the length of the rope. The fog that had settled at the bottom of the cave engulfed them as they fell.

[74]

Andrei looked over his shoulder and saw the shadowy forms of stalagmites rising to catch them.

"You're going to kill us!"

"Just one of us," Molnar laughed. "I'll let you guess which."

"*For fucks sakes*," Andrei yelped. He screamed as Molnar let go of the rope and they fell back into the mist, free-falling into darkness. The shapes of Xavier and the rest of the team dematerialized within the veil of fog as Andrei and Molnar plummeted towards the granite punji stakes below.

Andrei lost his grip on Molnar's back and hit the cave floor with a concussive *whump*. The impact winded him, but he was unharmed otherwise. Andrei groaned and rolled across the damp floor as the rest of the team landed softly around his splayed body. Molnar dusted himself off before scooping up Andrei by the collar of his khaki jacket.

"Have a little faith, Doc," Molnar said, slapping the mud and matted palm fronds from Andrei's jacket. "Gotta learn when to let go of the rope and land."

"You could have-," Andrei wheezed. "-Could have warned me."

"And you could have been a little more quiet on the way down," Konnor grunted, unclipping his carabineer.

"Right," Molnar said to Konnor, motioning to Andrei. "*I'm* the asshole. What did you expect, Doctor Wynn?"

"Death," Andrei groaned, popping his neck. "If I'm being honest."

Once Andrei was on his feet and pacing like usual, he took a pair of binoculars and started assessing his surroundings. He studied the vaulted ceiling and scanned the darkly glimmering rock walls, glistening wet with dew and dripping water. The floor of the cave was a maze of stalagmites ranging from three to fifteen feet high each. The surfaces of the conical spires sported patchworks of neon-green lichens and wooly, matted moss.

Palm plants and ferns took root across the floor of the cave, creating a miniature forest of undergrowth that blanketed the space between the natural obelisks. At the opposite end of the cavern, moonlight spilled forth from a second cave mouth. Even from across the chamber, Andrei could clearly see the stars blinking through the mist of the valley beyond through the jagged frame. Andrei lowered the binoculars and pointed to the forested hills outside, a vivid painting trapped within the dark rock wall.

"Looks like that's the only other exit," Andrei said. "We've got it trapped."

"For now," Xavier said. He took the headset from the radio strapped to his back and dialed the helicopter pilot. After listening to a beat of static, Xavier put the headset mic to his bearded lips and said, "We got it cornered. Yep. We need you to keep an eye on the cave entrance. Have Michael and Craig ready to blow apart any big bird that comes out."

"Roger that," the radio squawked.

"Alright," Xavier said, placing the headset back onto the radio. "Lights on."

There was a brief clatter of clicking and clacking switches. Pale white light shone from the end of every rifle barrel. Andrei took out a flashlight and played with the switch, shook the batteries in the chassis; it was dead.

"Andrei, stay behind Molnar," Xavier said. "Konnor, Syd; go to the cave entrance on the opposite end of the chamber and get ready to kill any bird that attempts to go in *or* out of the cave. Molnar, Andrei; you're with me. We're going to see if we can flush this bird out."

"Can't I stay behind Konnor or Syd?" Andrei asked. "I'm much less liable to die in a friendly-fire incident that way."

"Remington bucks back, not forward," Molnar said, pumping a slug into the chamber of his shotgun. "So long as you're not looking over my shoulder, you won't get hit by the recoil."

"Recoil isn't my concern," Andrei muttered.

Andrei looked around for some sort of support, but Syd and Konnor were already jogging through the shadows, their flashlights scattering and reforming across the faces of the stalagmites. Andrei sighed heavily as he followed Molnar and Xavier through the columns of vegetated rock. Their boot steps echoed throughout the chamber, and wind whistled through the fangs of the cave mouths. All else was silent within the mountain. The Father T. rex's thunderous roars echoed across the valley outside, shaking the walls of the cave. Droplets of water drizzled down from the ceiling onto Andrei's head.

"Better out there than in here," Andrei mumbled.

"Keep your eyes open," Xavier whispered over his shoulder. "That bird could be anywhere in here."

"Technically, the dromaeosaurids in the valley are more closely related to modern day birds than the quetzalcoatlus," Andrei said, stereotypically pushing his glasses up the bridge of his nose. It was a symbolic action of shielding himself from

[77]

his fears with scientific observation. A bad habit, and one that Xavier was well aware of.

"That's interesting and all," Xavier said. "But you don't want to think about utahraptors right now. You better knock on wood."

Andrei looked around; saw only rock and leaf litter. He shrugged.

"Superstitions are for the weak-minded," Andrei chuffed. He side-stepped a waist-high stalagmite and scurried back to Xavier. "Besides, if some utahraptors showed up, it might make our job easier. I've never seen a pack take on a Quetzalcoatlus, but I'd love to see the show."

"You say that now," Molnar grunted. "But think about what it did to those Kapro's."

There was a clatter of rocks, and Molnar and Xavier quickly directed their rifle barrels to the source of the sound. A nearby rock-wall had buckled and spilled forth wet slabs of slate. The beams of the men's flashlights climbed from the pile of rock to a ledge above. A pair of sapphire-scaled monitor lizards hissed as they scrambled away from the searching lights. Xavier frowned and lowered his rifle to his waist.

"Goddamned lizards," Xavier mumbled. "Goddamn all of 'em."

"Careful, Captain," Molnar whispered. "They'll hear you."

Xavier shook his head and brought his M16 back to his cheek. The beam of his flashlight speared into the empty space between two mossy pillars of rock, onto the scraggly black hide of the quetzalcoatlus shifting through the darkness. A bloodied beak swung through the beam of light, nearly knocking the rifle from Xavier's hands.

Xavier pulled the trigger of his M16 and back-pedaled away as the muzzle flare from his rifle lit the body of the fleeing quetzalcoatlus in a blinking strobe. The pterosaur vanished amongst the fog-draped rows of stalagmites as quickly as it had appeared. The steam generated by Xavier's panting breath filtered through his beard. The plinking of dripping water returned with the absence of echoing rifle reports.

Xavier scanned the shadowy pillars of stone with his rifle's barrel-light. He could hear the quetzalcoatlus shambling through the cavern, the folds of its wing membranes audibly scraping against wet rock.

Xavier tilted his head to the walkie-talkie strapped to his shoulder.

"Konnor, Syd, are you at the adjacent cave mouth?"

The walkie talkie hissed. Static buzzed around Xavier's head.

"Yes sir, Captain Wise," Konnor responded through the crackling frequency. "Did you see the quetzalcoatlus? We saw your gunshots, heard the animal. It's here?"

"Its home," Xavier gravely said. "Keep your rifles ready. We're going to chase it out to you. Over."

"Roger that," Konnor said. The static ceased.

Xavier tightened his grip around the barrel of his M16 as he led Molnar and Andrei further into the labyrinth of stalagmites. Their boot-steps echoed quietly through the lichen-traced columns, causing the sounds to be scattered further into the darkness. It sounded to Xavier as if an additional dozen men were walking through the cave, scrambling around in the shadows beyond the reach of their lights. It caused the hackles on his neck to rise like a cat on edge. He released his tension in a mighty gust of vaporous mist; a sigh suspended in the dank air. He had to wave aside the miniature cloud with a free hand just to see.

As Xavier waved the hanging mist away from his eyes, the black obelisk before him suddenly uprooted itself from the cave floor. Xavier screamed and opened fire, peppering the quetzalcoatlus's feathered back as the animal scuttled away, its knuckles splashing through the puddles on the cave floor.

"Molnar, look alive," Xavier barked.

Molnar ran past Xavier and fired a slug from his Remington at the fleeing silhouette of the quetzalcoatlus. The animal shouldered past a stalagmite, topping the stone. Xavier rolled away to avoid being struck by the falling rock. Molnar feigned around him and shot a second slug at the quetzalcoatlus. The muzzle flare illuminated the quetzalcoatlus's lanky neck and shambling forelimbs. The creature was struck in the hind leg by Molnar's slug, and it howled as it buckled to the floor.

Before Molnar could fire another round at the Quetzalcoatlus, the animal spun around and struck Molnar's chest with the broad side of its beak. The impact spun Molnar on his heels and he struck a stalagmite face-first. Xavier caught Molnar before he could hit the floor and quickly dragged him away from the crawling quetzalcoatlus.

Xavier's rifle was hanging by its shoulder strap, so he couldn't get a clear shot at the animal as it charged. He could hear the creature dragging itself forward, stumbling, groaning through its beak as its barbed tongue unfurled. Xavier found the prehensile tongue lunging through the beam of his barrel-light, and he tripped backwards over a knee-high stalagmite.

Xavier instinctively rolled sideways just as the quetzalcoatlus lunged forward, slamming the tip of its beak against the granite floor. Xavier heard a *snap* like a tree-limb breaking in half, and the quetzalcoatlus wailed in agony. The force of the animal's pained cries caused the stalactites above to shake in their roots. Bats squealed and squeaked as they flew down from the ceiling. Xavier scrambled back onto his feet, heaving Molnar up beside him.

"On your feet, Molnar!" Xavier barked.

Molnar clambered to his feet, swinging the Remington high so that the barrel-light from the shotgun blurred across the quetzalcoatlus. The carnivore was back-pedaling away into the darkness; the keratinous sheath that covered its beak had splintered at the end of its snout. Slick, brackish blood drained from the splintered cracks in the quetzalcoatlus's beak as Molnar's light skimmed across its face. The quetzalcoatlus honked and lunged towards Molnar's light. With a quick tug of his trigger finger, Molnar fired the Remington and blasted off the tip of the quetzalcoatlus's beak.

The quetzalcoatlus trumpeted in agony as it stumbled away from the men. Molnar and Xavier opened fire, chasing the animal through the cavern of mossy pillars. They moved through the darkness as apparitions, no longer predator and prey, but equals. The quetzalcoatlus could have just as easily dispatched of Stalker Force as it had the kaprosuchus rogues, but the tables were turning.

The agonized predator finally felt fear.

[81]

The quetzalcoatlus whimpered and whinnied in pain through its fractured beak. Blood drained from the splintered keratin as the quetzalcoatlus stumbled away from the shouting men of Stalker Force. The quetzalcoatlus understood its way around the nesting site it had shared with its mate, navigated it without any difficulty. The pterosaur was tall enough that it could easily see the adjacent cave mouth across the chamber. The quetzalcoatlus began to move more forcefully, propelling itself forward with its forelimbs while its wounded leg dragged behind it. The moonlight flooding the cave was a sign of escape; a chance for survival.

An agonized predator was waiting for the quetzalcoatlus.

Syd Kinane stood before the cave mouth as the quetzalcoatlus rushed forward. The quetzalcoatlus had no plan, no strategy; it simply equated the starlight of the night sky with another day alive. The animal didn't have the intuition to know that its escape was futile. It was running head-first into a trap, the oldest kind man had ever used; a strategy that had been implemented since Homo Sapien hunted the mammoth to extinction.

Syd hefted his M60 to his shoulder and pulled the trigger. The heavy machine gun screamed through the cavern, as loud as lightning, and the quetzalcoatlus' torso was churned to liquid by live-fire. The quetzalcoatlus staggered forward, incapable of stopping its momentum, and crashed face-down at Syd and Konnor's feet. The quetzalcoatlus attempted to drag itself forward to throw itself out of the cave, but Syd and Konnor blocked its passage with a wall of hailing lead. The pterosaur's body crumpled to the dampened floor as the rifles roared.

"Ease off," Konnor shouted, taking his finger off the trigger. "Hold your fire. I think its dead"

[82]

Syd shouldered past Konnor and stood over the dying quetzalcoatlus. The animal's eyes were bloodshot, rolling wetly like oil within its sunken eye sockets. As the quetzalcoatlus's pupils found Syd's face, trying to transmit some sense of empathy, Syd raised his machete. He stooped over the groaning pterosaur and tightened his hold on the blade.

"Syd," Konnor said. "What are you-"

Syd swung the machete down, hacking the blade half-way through the middle of the groaning animal's giraffe-like neck. The quetzalcoatlus retched, the prehensile tongue grasping feebly from its shattered beak. Syd swung the machete again, chopping cleanly through the discs of vertebrae. Once the animal's head was completely severed, Syd buried his machete into the eye socket. Syd was panting softly with his exertion, his arms hanging loose from his broad, heaving shoulders.

"Jesus Christ, Syd-"

"Cool it, Jung," Syd croaked without looking back. "Don't spoil this for me."

Konnor curled his lip in disgust, but didn't speak otherwise.

"Things are different here," Syd said, withdrawing his machete. He tilted the blade through the moonlight that flowed into the cave. "This ain't even Vietnam anymore. This is a safari park. There's no shame here in butchering what you kill."

"Okay, whatever you say," Konnor said, raising his hands in compliance. "I didn't see anything."

The tapping of rubber soles against the floor announced the return of Xavier, Molnar, and Andrei. Konnor saluted as they approached, half-way covering

[83]

his eyes to shield himself from the biting beams of their barrel-lights. When the group converged around the body of the dead quetzalcoatlus, they shared wary eye contact. There was no doubt to what had happened; they had worked together to ensure the extinction of a man-eating species.

What danger remained lay out of sight as the men returned to their helicopter. When the helicopter lifted off from the mountain, their floodlights surveyed the walls of the peak. They found no nests, no shelters, and no additional quetzalcoatlus. There didn't appear to be a successor to the throne of the valley's sky. The king of the valley winds, the White Whale of Syd's pursuits, died alone with no nest to claim within its home-turned-tomb.

The quetzalcoatlus's kin had fled the valley long ago.

KILLER WHALE

The valley fell silent as the sun descended behind the western mountain walls. Herds of triceratops and parasaurolophus ended their songs from the shelter of banyan-rimmed floodplains. Starlight shone on the silken feather pelts of deinonychus clinging to the highest tree tops; their shrill siren calls cutting short with the appearance of a full moon. The mobs of kaprosuchus that galloped along the waterways became sluggish as the cool night wind chilled their cold blood. The night belonged to the utahraptors of the valley; even the Father T. rex stayed close to his mate's side when the scent of the lethal dromaeosaurids filtered through their bamboo grove.

In a lone clearing of trampled vegetation, a small family of utahraptors began their nightly rituals. The hunting party, a group of four males led by their alpha, chirruped as they sprinted through the undergrowth in search of prey. Their micro-colony was a faction of Sobek Colony that had broken away for better chances of survival. The hunting party was preying upon the Army Corps of Engineers; the same source of food that fed so many other micro-colonies of utahraptors.

Nearly all of the utahraptor micro-colonies had been destroyed.

A pair of beta male utahraptors remained at the nesting site to protect the two females; the matriarch and a beta female. The two males grunted to one another as they circled the perimeter, constantly searching the darkness with their amber-glowing eyes. The matriarch was nestled upon her clutch, protecting the eggs from the cutting winds with her shaggy coat of feathers. The beta female was busy grooming herself, nipping through her protofeathers to get at the ticks and fleas beneath.

[85]

One of the beta male utahraptors stopped his rounds when he detected a sound from the east. He paused mid-step, one leg raised to his hip while balancing on the other like a flamingo. The beta male cocked his head and hummed like a kakapo parrot, a low rumbling rising from his maned throat. The other beta male noticed the distress of the first and paused as well, puffing up his torso feathers in a show of agitation.

The beta male that had detected the sound first was an older male, with scars criss-crossing through the crest of feathers on the back of his skull. The elder beta male groaned as he allowed his other foot to fall. The beta grunted at the matriarch, then turned towards the east. The younger beta male chirruped inquisitively, cocking his head from left to right. The scarred beta silenced the younger beta utahraptor with a hearty chuff. The vocalization was a clear directive to the young beta male; *stay*.

As the elder beta ventured into the forest, the younger beta male returned to the matriarch and beta female. They were positioned in the center of the clearing, each curled in a six-foot wide nest of packed mud. The beta female chirped and flexed her clawed forefingers. When the beta male was within ten feet of the Matriarch's nest, she bared her teeth and growled vehemently.

Even though the beta male was the only animal there to defend the females, they wouldn't allow him anywhere near their eggs. It was common for male utahraptors to cannibalize the eggs of a harem when contesting the alpha for dominance of the colony.

Several minutes passed as the beta male continued his rounds along the tree-line. There were no sounds from the surrounding forest; no animal dared to make a noise when the apex predators of the valley were near. The absence of the

[86]

older beta brought a sense of menace to the silence for the three utahraptors remaining at the nesting site. The beta male felt his instinctual senses heighten with a rush of paranoia-fueled adrenaline. He was constantly anticipating the clatter of branches breaking or the vocalizations of the scarred beta utahraptor, but no sound ever came.

Only the wind made itself known to the utahraptors.

The beta male sniffed the air; the nesting site was downwind of the scarred older male, wherever he was within the jungle. The beta male could smell the other male somewhere in the forest, but it seemed as if he had remained in the same position he had ventured. Why hadn't he changed direction, or at least communicated his position? The beta male whimpered softly, nervously fanning the flight feathers along his forearms. He yipped like a dog at the two females, bobbing his head in the direction of the scarred beta male's wind-swept scent.

The young beta male utahraptor trotted across the clearing and ducked into the foliage that filled the understory of the forest. The night was dark, but his vision was as keen and acute as a jaguar. Nothing could hide from the master ambush predator.

After running for a hundred yards, the beta male was struck fully by the scent of his pack-mate. The beta male slowed his trot, jerking his head back as he inhaled deeply through his pulsing nostrils. He groaned in distress; the smell of his pack-mate was soured with a scent similar to that of an infant utahraptor's favorite meal.

Spilled organs.

[87]

The beta male utahraptor scanned the forest floor, sniffing through the foliage with his head held low to the ground. After jabbing his leathery snout through several plumes of palm plants, he found a shining wet fruit lying in an expansive footprint filled with blood and bile. The curious beta male took a chance to lick the fresh organ, probing the valves and arteries with his tongue.

The beta male retched and bounced back to his full height. He cocked his head at the still-bleeding utahraptor heart and chirruped anxiously. A wary growl sifted through his serrated fangs. When he discovered the source of the organ, a distressed groan was relinquished from his voluminous chest.

The scarred beta male utahraptor was lying amongst the palm plants, bleeding and beaten to a grisly pulp. The freshly slaughtered carcass was covered in long, deep lacerations that revealed glistening white bone in the moonlight. The dead beta utahraptor's winged forearms appeared to have been ripped from their sockets, discarded on the forest floor beside the body. The beta male stopped surveying the corpse of his pack-mate when he looked beyond the carcass's contorted neck.

The utahraptor's head had been crushed under-foot.

The beta male hissed like a feral cat with alarm, jerking his head from left to right to see into the forest beyond. He caught no sign of any other animals in the forest. No other sounds filtered through the air other than the dry rasp of palm fronds being stirred by the wind. The beta male sniffed deeply, but that only carried the scent of his eviscerated pack-mate to his palette. The beta male retched, spreading his jaws wide, and a pool of saliva found its way from his lower jaw to the forest floor below, where it splashed atop the tip of a curled tail.

The tail suddenly slipped away from the utahraptor.

The beta male barked in surprise as the feathered tail was pulled through the underbrush. The foliage roiled around the beta male, and an immense black-bodied theropod rose from the undergrowth several feet away. The tail of the animal swept through the air, brushing shaggy proto-feathers across the beta male's face. The beta male utahraptor squealed out fearfully and leapt away as the silhouetted theropod towered before it.

The beta male's eyes darted across the features of the unfamiliar predator; it was much larger than a utahraptor, but smaller than the Father T. rex. The dinosaur was a yutyrannus, a smaller relative of the Tyrannosaur family with a shaggy black coat of protofeathers that made it nearly imperceptible within the darkness. The yutyrannus opened its bone-crushing maw and howled at the beta male, causing the smaller carnivore to turn and flee.

The yutyrannus spread its long, muscular forelimbs and chased after the beta male utahraptor, crashing through the understory vegetation. A second yutyrannus heard the vocalizations of its mate and joined the chase, plodding on thick, stocky legs that snapped through the thin-trucked sapling trees.

The beta male momentarily glanced back at the pursuing theropods as he sprinted away, but he only caught a glimpse of the nocturnal predators' crimson eyes, encased in ghastly pools of pallid white scales. The yutyrannus ducked their heads low, allowing their red-rimmed cranial crests to carve a path through the forest.

The beta male utahraptor faced forward and dove through the tree-line that enclosed the nesting site. The females shrieked in alarm as the beta male landed nimbly between them. The matriarch was about to nip at the beta male when she noticed the crashing trees thundering throughout the forest beyond. The beta male

[89]

stood between the females and the tumultuous jungle, splaying his arms in a defensive posture. The females wrapped their arms around their clutches and craned their necks back to see past the beta male.

The chaotic din beyond the tree-line ceased. Whatever path the yutyrannus had been making had been cut short. The beta male utahraptor lifted his head, trying to smell the two larger theropods, but he was out of luck. If a human scientist had examined the yutyrannus, they would have discovered that the yutyrannus possessed specialized protofeathers that trapped their scents and concealed them from their prey.

The yutyrannus were as good as invisible to the utahraptors.

Clattering tree branches captured the beta male's attention; a palm tree toppled on the opposite end of the clearing. The beta male twisted his neck around as a behemoth's roar blasted through the tree-line.

The beta male turned just as a yutyrannus charged into the clearing, its head held low and jaws stretching wide to catch the matriarch. The beta male howled and pounced onto the yutyrannus from the side, kicking his sickle-shaped toe claws at the larger theropod's flank.

The beta male's claws were quickly entangled in the yutyrannus's ragged pelt. The yutyrannus arched its head back, eyes burning crimson within the white pits of its orbital sockets. The beta male shrieked and slashed his forearm talons at the yutyrannus's throat, but he couldn't cut through the larger animal's thick mane. The yutyrannus howled and slammed its jaws shut over the beta male's shoulder.

The yutyrannus's five-inch long fangs broke through the beta male's shoulder as if the utahraptor's bones were porcelain. The beta male shrieked as the

[90]

yutyrannus jerked its head back, rending the utahraptor's forelimb from its socket. Blood jettisoned from the wound as the beta male crashed down between the yutyrannus and the female utahraptors. The other yutyrannus was sauntering forth from the opposite end of the clearing, its long arms flexing with vile energy.

The hunt was on.

The beta male utahraptor yowled as the first yutyrannus kicked him in the stomach. The beta male went rolling, and the long gashes crossing his abdomen split open. Slippery intestines and bulbous organs blossomed from the beta male's lacerated gut. The beta male shrieked as he dragged himself towards the female utahraptors, still driven by instinctual need to protect them at all cost. The yutyrannus followed close behind, popping the beta male's trailing organs underfoot.

The matriarch utahraptor was shrieking at the yutyrannus, attempting to scare it away from the beta male. The other female stood between her clutch and the second yutyrannus.

The beta male attempted to climb to his feet, but the first yutyrannus brought its foot down on his neck, crushing the vertebrae like glass against the floor of the clearing. The matriarch squealed in shock as bloody sputum sprayed from the slain beta male's jaws. Before the matriarch utahraptor could react, the yutyrannus slammed its jaws around her head, snapping her skull in half.

The lone surviving female utahraptor remained with her eggs despite the death of her pack mates. She arched her head back and screamed, filling the valley with her call for help. The hunting party would come back when they heard her cries, but how soon was a mystery. There wasn't a way out for the female other than running or fighting, but she wouldn't survive by protecting her nest.

[91]

The female utahraptor's instincts would doom her.

A yutyrannus sauntered past the female utahraptor and seized the beta male in its jaws. The theropod was going to drag the carcasses away from the nest. It was in the nature of yutyrannus to systematically kill any competition in their chosen niche. This behavior was similar to the hunting of sharks by killer whales; an intelligent predator taking out threats to their survival before the threat could multiply.

The female utahraptor howled in anguish as the yutyrannus dragged away the carcasses of her pack-mates. With her back turned, the female utahraptor was an easy target for the other yutyrannus. The second yutyrannus pounced onto the female from behind, burying its three-inch long talons into the female's hips. The female utahraptor shrieked in pain and attempted to leap away, but she was pinned in place by the larger animal's powerful forearms.

The yutyrannus caught the female utahraptor's neck in its jaws and bit down, easily severing the head from the spinal column. The female utahraptor's head fell to the ground as the yutyrannus tugged its teeth through the animal's flesh. The yutyrannus roared victoriously as it crushed the severed head underfoot, raising its horns to the moon above. The pair of yutyrannus howled at one another, drowning the echoing screams of the hunting party attempting to communicate with their fallen pack mates.

Slaughtering the adult utahraptors was only a small part of their ritual.

After dragging the bodies away from the nest, the yutyrannus set about investigating the egg clutches. The shaggy-coated carnivores lowered their white-rimmed eyes to the nests to examine the hatchlings within. There were a few infant utahraptors in each clutch. The infant utahraptors clambered over the eggs of their

[92]

unhatched siblings, squeaking like baby birds in search of a parental offering of food. The yutyrannus glowered over the downy infants, their ruby pupils gleaming.

The yutyrannus started by eating each of the infants; they scooped the little utahraptors up in their jaws and chewed the animals to a pulp between their serrated fangs. After eating the last crying infant, the yutyrannus set about crushing all of the eggs. They kicked their talons through the nests, splashing yolk and developing fetuses beneath their splayed feet. Once both nests were decimated, the yutyrannus grunted to one another and returned to the darkness of the forest beyond the tree-line.

The alpha utahraptor's hunting party arrived within minutes. When they discovered the nesting site was devoid of life, the alpha and his subordinates went searching through the forest for their missing pack-mates. The alpha led the way, criss-crossing through the foliage while moaning in distress. Wherever he looked, he found only splashed blood and viscera.

The alpha utahraptor didn't see the yutyrannus until it was too late.

BILE

With the quetzalcoatlus slain and the monsoon season withering to an end, Stalker Force redirected all of their time and focus into locating the nesting site of Sobek Colony. Xavier Wise and Andrei Wynn believed they had pin-pointed the location of Nesting-Site B within the western half of the valley, nestled halfway up the sloping mountain wall amongst resplendent ficus and banyan trees.

The Army Corps of Engineers had spent a few difficult months repairing damage to the electric perimeters that lined the crenulated mountaintops. Several workmen had gone missing from their tents in the middle of the night despite the presence of additional security forces. The utahraptor footprints that led from the Army Corps camps to the interior of the valley marked the trail for Stalker Force.

After a few rounds of reconnaissance, tracking footprints, feathers and acrid white dung, Stalker Force managed to narrow down nesting site B to a remote enclave nestled between the forks of a stream running through the sloping forest hills. Once Xavier and Andrei annotated the forked stream on their topographical map, they set out for the hunt.

"Up the tree, Andrei," Xavier said.

Andrei craned his head back to see the full height of the ficus looming overhead. The vine-laden tree had an expansive canopy that leaned just far enough from the near-vertical slope to provide a vantage of the nesting site downhill. The lowest boughs of the tree drooped heavily nearly thirty feet above Andrei's head. The mushroom-capped tree top was a veritable hive of twisting branches, tangled vines and wet, waxy leaves. Stagnant drops of water sluiced down as the canopy shifted. Andrei tried to peer through the canopy to spot the monkeys he heard hooting and hollering within, but it was as infeasible as staring through a boulder.

A pebble fell from within the ficus canopy, bouncing off of branches on its passage down to the roots of the ficus, where it ricocheted off of a half-buried stygimoloch skull.

"Well," Andrei said. "It beats being on the ground with utahraptors."

"And utahraptor hunters," Molnar grinned, nudging Andrei. "Right?"

"*Dah*," Andrei nodded emphatically. "Far away from you, comrade."

"What a shock," Syd Kinane spoke up. He had his M60 slung over his shoulder, flak jacket open to reveal his thick trunk. "The cowardly communist hides again. Just as nature intended."

"He's not hiding," Craig Jacobs, the sniper, said. He slapped Andrei on the shoulder as he walked past, M14 in hand. "He's with us, right Michael?"

Michael Waters, the stocky African-American spotter, followed Craig to the base of the ficus. He glanced at Andrei as he passed, raising his brow judiciously as he skimmed over the young scientist's rail-thin arms, track-marked and scarred.

"Better hope not," Michael said.

Andrei looked at Xavier, who shrugged. When Andrei turned back to Michael and Craig, they were already scaling the rope-thick vines all the way up to the lowest bough. Michael reached the top first, swinging his legs around the thick branch. Craig glanced down at Andrei as he heaved himself up beside Michael.

"Want any help, doc?"

"Sure," Andrei said, grabbing onto a vine and pulling to test its strength. "Psychiatric; therapeutic; help putting me out of my misery. Did I ever mention I'm scared of heights?"

"We can help with the last one," Michael drawled.

Andrei climbed the vine as quickly as he could without looking down. When he was finally within their reach, Craig and Michael grabbed Andrei by the shoulders and pulled him onto the branch. Andrei immediately felt vertigo; gravity crept up his nerve endings like ethereal fingers, gripping his core, pulling him down. Andrei yelped deliriously as he swung his arms to fight the vertigo, but Craig grabbed him by the collar of his khaki jacket and steadied him.

"Easy does it, killer," Craig said. "You don't want to pull us down with you."

"You don't want to pull me down," Michael said. "I'll bury you where I land."

"Got it," Andrei said, nodding and exhaling tremulously. "Don't fall. Sound advice, comrades."

Andrei's bespectacled eyes appeared to vibrate as he attempted to study every inch of the canopy interior. It was as if he had entered a bubble constructed of a trailing network of vines and wiry branches, concealed from the surrounding rainforest by a shroud of stiff leaves. The sun was at its pinnacle position above the valley, but scarce light managed to fight through the ficus tree's thick crown of jade locks. The monsoons had ended only a week ago, but it seemed to Andrei as if the ficus had refused to relinquish any of the rainwater trapped within its canopy.

"Come on, doc," Craig said. "Team's getting in position. Time to move."

[96]

Andrei nodded without thinking. He watched as Craig and Michael shimmied along the length of the bough and climbed up to a higher branch. Andrei held his breath and followed suit, ignoring every instinct in his body to check what height he was ascending to. After climbing and twisting through the lattice work of wooden tendrils, the trio found a safe branch that cut through the canopy and emerged into the open air.

Andrei tried to distract himself from the mild tremors rippling through the branch. Their efforts climbing had been rewarded with an expansive view of the forked creek below. To Andrei's surprise, they were still in the understory; the higher canopy constructed by patriarchal banyans and kapok trees fully suppressed the mid-day sun and sheltered the undergrowth in a shade as thick and dark as night. Waist-high rhododendron and king ferns concealed the broken shale clearing between the opposing streams.

In the carpeted clearing between the gurgling streams, the carcass of a slain sauropod lay rotting within a ring of mud-packed nests. It was difficult to tell what species the immense herbivorous dinosaur had been, as weeks of rainfall had eroded the cadaver to a disheveled pile of bone and spoiled grey gristle.

Andrei's curiosity was piqued; could the utahraptors have worked collectively to bring the carcass to that spot, or had they herded it to their home and slaughtered it? He reasoned that the stream could have washed the body downstream from during the monsoon season.

Another day, another stream of questions without answers.

Despite the presence of a carcass and nests, the site was otherwise empty. Andrei frowned as he pulled the walkie-talkie from his backpack. He watched the

[97]

clearing until Xavier's head surfaced above the king ferns before speaking into the mic.

"It looks like they may have relocated during the wet season," Andrei whispered. "What do you say? Pack up and call for the evac, or wait and see if they return?"

Xavier grumbled through the static in Andrei's ear.

"They're always a step ahead, Andrei. I'm starting to think you're playing for the wrong team."

Andrei laughed; a cough coming from the bottom of his throat.

"I wish. Do you think the yutyrannus killed off Sobek Colony?"

"If we're lucky," the walkie-talkie crackled.

"We never are," Andrei said. From his vantage point, he could see the helmets of Stalker Force punctuating the rhododendron and fern fronds like half-concealed stones. Andrei watched as Xavier hesitated at the edge of the nesting site.

"See any utah's?" Xavier asked, his smooth voice buzzing through the air.

"Tell 'im no," Michael said, glancing at Andrei.

"No," Andrei said. "You're clear."

Xavier and the rest of Stalker Force eddied out of the vegetation and into the muddy clearing. Xavier covered his mouth as he circled the long-forgotten carcass in the center of the nesting site. An amoebic black cloud of insects rose from

[98]

the pools of yellowing liquid fat. Andrei heard Molnar gag from below. Molnar briefly crested the rhododendron, turning away to double over and vomit.

"That'll get you good and fucked," Michael whispered. Craig chuckled beside him on the branch.

"How much you wanna bet he tastes it," Craig said, elbowing Andrei.

Andrei flinched and slapped his hands around the branch for stability. A powerful tremor rippled through the earth, causing the ficus to bounce and sway. Andrei held a scream tight behind his teeth as he held on tight to the tree limb. Craig and Michael were momentarily alarmed, touching the branch as they looked around for the cause of the quake.

"The Father T. rex?" Craig asked, looking at Andrei.

Andrei shook his head violently.

"It better not be, for our sake."

There was a flash of light from the forest beyond the clearing. The trees swayed and creaked gently as they were brushed aside. Plodding footsteps resounded throughout the open air. Down below, Xavier and the other men of Stalker Force quickly crowded around the fetid sauropod remains for cover. They started pointing, whispering to one another as a great silhouetted leviathan pushed its way into the clearing.

"What's this thing called, Andrei?" the radio whispered.

A living member of the dead sauropod's species was meandering into the clearing. It was what would often be described by children as a 'long neck dinosaur'.

This diminutive relative of ancient titans like Diplodocus and Apatosaurus was scarcely larger than the triceratops that roamed the valley, but it easily towered over the cowering men of Stalker Force. The dinosaur's serpentine neck supported a translucent, fleshy sail intersected by meter-long neural spines. The flaccid membranes swelled as the animal breathed, and the spaces between the neural spines pulsed with soft green bioluminescence.

"Amargasaurus," Andrei exhaled into the walkie-talkie. "Keep your trigger fingers loose. It's not going to hurt anybody so long as you don't antagonize it. Just get away from the carcass and leave it be, or sit back and enjoy the show."

"The show?" Craig asked, looking at Andrei.

"Did anybody even read their bestiaries?" Andrei grumbled.

"The what?"

"The field guides I made for the team," Andrei hissed.

"Pretty pictures," Michael said from further down the branch. "Too many words."

"Thanks," Andrei seethed. "But there's barely more than *forty pages*."

"Forty pages too many," Michael said, clearing his throat.

Andrei rolled his eyes and turned to watch the amargasaurus. The lone long-necked leviathan lowered its miniscule head to investigate the bones of its fallen kin. As the muddy-eyed titan sniffed the malformed carcass, the amargasaurus's sail began to swirl and light more urgently with color. Moody blues and sickly pale yellow flashed throughout the membranous sail as the amargasaurus moaned in

[100]

distress. The sound was resonant with pain, a mournful song like a beached whale crying to return to its ancestral waters.

"Spooky," Craig said. "Think it knows?"

"Maybe," Andrei said. "I've never seen an amargasaurus act like this before. I don't think there's more than a handful of these amargasaurus in the valley. They tend to stay hidden from all of the other dinosaurs. They don't have much in terms of defense other than their size, but even the utahraptors are big enough to pick them off. I'm surprised there's any left at all."

Effervescent lantern lights flashed and bobbed from the darkness beyond the abandoned nesting site. Andrei saw the tops of Stalker Force's helmets rotate as the men tried to sight all of the approaching Amargasaurus. Three more of the titanic quadrupeds came shuffling shyly from the jungle to see their slaughtered species-mate. The sauropods paid no attention to the soldiers cowering amongst the remains of the carcass.

The collected group of Amargasaurus began to pace around the pile of bone and rot, swaying as they delicately placed each step. Their moans and howls of anguish filled the valley like the swan songs of dying pagan gods. Andrei watched as the bioluminescent sails flashed blue, green, rosy pink and neon black. A halo of water-color light swirled around the dead Amargasaurus, and within the rainbow orbit sat the perplexed men of Stalker Force.

"They know," Andrei said softly. "Like elephants."

"Elephants?" Michael repeated, looking at Andrei.

"Elephants recognize their dead," Andrei said. "Some specialists have observed elephants performing a similar ritual when they find the carcasses of other

[101]

elephants. I highly doubt the Amargasaurus possess the same depth of understanding and intuition as pachyderms, but hell, look at it. They understand something of significance, to some extent."

The bioluminescent halo tightened around Stalker Force. The Amargasaurus family began to swing their tails as they marched, grunting and guffawing into the open air. Some stamped their feet powerfully against the earth while others took furtive chances to examine the canopy overhead. Andrei felt momentarily perplexed; was this a ritual upon the recognition of death, or was it an act of defense?

"Look up," Xavier's voice buzzed from the radio.

Andrei raised his head to the upper-story canopy of the banyans and kapok trees. Iridescent blue-black feathered dromaeosaurids were crawling through the latticework of branches, hopping lower and lower towards the understory canopy. Andrei felt his mouth dry up with the release of fresh adrenaline. The pack of small carnivores clambering down towards Stalker Force were deinonychus; arboreal hunters closely related to the utahraptors they had been trying to find.

"Bad," Andrei stammered. "Bad, bad, not good-"

"What," Craig said, glancing at Andrei. "Where-"

There was a high-pitched scream from above, cutting through the dissonant roaring of the Amargasaurus. A streak of sparkling blue feathers speared through the air and collided with Craig, tossing him off of the branch and further into the ficus tree's canopy. Andrei screamed as the branch bounced and he was thrown into the air. He fell onto the branch face-first, breaking his nose but otherwise clinging for dear life, wrapping his limbs around the gnarled bark.

[102]

Michael climbed across the branch and pulled Andrei back into a sitting position. They turned around and started crawling back into the canopy. Craig's screams caterwauled throughout the labyrinthine hive. Andrei struggled to see where Craig had landed. A single misplaced step could result in a bone-breaking fall. He could hear a dozen of the nimble-bodied deinonychus crashing through the ficus tree's canopy, cackling and cawing to one another as their claws stripped through vines and vegetation.

Andrei tasted bile.

BILE II

The ficus tree that overlooked utahraptor nesting site B roiled and shook as an entire pack of deinonychus elegantly writhed and twisted through its tangled canopy. Andrei Wynn was hyperventilating as he struggled to keep up with Michael Waters in their search for Craig Jacobs. It was dark, claustrophobic, and wet with cold dew. Andrei shimmied down a bough after Michael, penetrating the shadows and foliage with a hand stretched out, grasping for hand-holds. Michael pulled apart a weave of branches ahead and slipped through to further darkness.

Andrei held his breath as he clambered through the net of snaking tree-limbs. He tried to pull himself through to the other side, but sinuous vines gripped his khaki uniform like lecherous tendrils. Andrei's heart lunged into his throat and he choked, momentarily stricken with fear. Down below the Amargasaurus were stamping their feet and braying around the nest site, their bellowing calls shaking the ficus in its roots. Andrei dug his nails into the bark of the branch he was clinging to.

Everything within Andrei's sight was moving; it was impossible for him to tell where any of the deinonychus were. He could hear their claws clacking against bark, their razor-edged teeth clicking as they snapped their jaws hungrily. A sudden weight struck the opposite end of the branch Andrei was crawling on, and he froze as the bough bobbed hazardly. He started to panic, viciously tearing at the stems digging through his uniform. Andrei felt something snatch him by the shoulder and he was wrenched through the trap.

Andrei screamed as he fell forward, but he was quickly halted by Michael's stocky frame. Michael shoved Andrei back and pointed to a branch below. Before Andrei could even suck in a breath, Michael was already swinging off their branch to the next branch below. Michael glanced up at Andrei without speaking, motioning with a single hand to jump down.

Andrei was trembling and hyperventilating breathlessly. He turned as the clustered branches Michael had wrenched him through began to shift. The reptilian snout of a deinonychus shot forward through the net, jaws snapping and glimmering eyes locked on Andrei. The deinonychus shrieked, its vocalization like nails grinding through a chalkboard, as it slithered towards him. Andrei cried out and slipped off of the branch.

Claws whistled past Andrei's face as he fell and struck the lower branch gut-first. His head swung forward as pain exploded throughout his abdomen. There was a scream from above, and the light weight of the deinonychus struck the small of Andrei's spine. Andrei shrieked, clawing forward without thinking, and he slid head-first off of the branch. The deinonychus squealed as it leapt off of Andrei to the safety of a higher limb of the ficus.

Andrei spun through the air, leaves and branches crackling around his body as he tumbled. He reached out blindly, groping for something to stop his rapid descent, and he managed to catch a vine in both hands. The momentum of the fall continued to drag Andrei down the length of stringy cirrus. His palms burned as he tightened his grip; his nails quickly chipped and broke apart as he buried them into the fleshy fiber.

A hand gripped Andrei's shirt collar and his descent was cut short. Michael heaved Andrei up onto a wide bough beside him as another deinonychus pounced onto a branch overhead. Michael fired several rounds at the deinonychus, driving the carnivore back into hiding. Screams ripped through Andrei's ear drums; he looked towards the bloodcurdling howl.

"Jesus," Andrei choked, covering his mouth. "Jesus-"

Craig was splayed at the opposite end of the branch with his back up against the trunk and a deinonychus straddling his chest. Craig screeched as the glittering black-feathered dromaeosaurid rabidly lacerated his torso with its swinging fore-claws. He raised a hand to halt a blow to his throat only for the deinonychus's talons to swipe off his digits. Another deinonychus was perched on a branch over his head, gnawing at his bare scalp.

Andrei could see stripes of pale bone emerging from beneath the deinonychus's grinding fangs. The deinonychus on Craig's chest stopped swinging its forearms and started gnawing at Craig's throat. As it chewed through Craig's Adam's apple, the deinonychus kicked his gut, splitting open his abdomen with its scything toe claws.

Andrei was numb; Craig made eye contact, but only a gurgling moan managed to escape through his lacerated throat. The deinonychus paused as it observed the blood bubbling from the base of Craig's neck. It puffed its feathers up, glancing up and down Craig's face with its inquisitive avian eyes. Craig momentarily looked into the pupils of his killer. There was a pause as the men of Stalker Force shouted from below, the amargasaurus still braying, the other deinonychus shrieking and cawing.

Andrei stared vacantly as the deinonychus severed Craig's lower jaw with a swipe of its fore-claws. Gunshots cracked from behind Andrei, and he glanced mindlessly over his shoulder at Michael. The sniper was taking shots at the deinonychus, screaming for Andrei to get out of his line of sight. When Andrei remained frozen for five more agonizing seconds, Michael lost his patience and fired a round past Andrei's face, jolting him back to conscious reality.

[106]

Andrei ducked down and hugged the branch as bullets snapped over his head. The deinonychus on top of Craig shrieked from the opposite end of the branch. Andrei felt the tree limb bobbing beneath him as the deinonychus leapt from its perch. Feathers brushed the back of Andrei's head as the small carnivore sailed over him, tackling into Michael and down through the canopy.

Andrei was deaf to the *whump* of their impact.

The men of Stalker Force were screaming and shouting from below. The rest of the deinonychus were converging on Andrei's position. He could already hear a few of them raking their talons through Craig's masticated corpse. Andrei reached for a vine without thinking, overwhelmed by the chaotic din he was trapped within. A deinonychus snapped its jaws around his boot and his mental clarity returned with a rip-tide of mind-rending terror.

Andrei screamed as he slid down the length of the vine. He didn't care how fast he was falling, how far he was dropping, what would happen to him when he landed. The deinonychus were pouncing from branch to branch after him. Andrei kicked through the bottom of the ficus tree's canopy and saw the ground rushing up to him from twenty feet below. He dug his boot heels into the vine, clamped his teeth around it, and contorted his body to provide as much fiery friction as possible.

The vine stopped ten feet above the forest floor.

Andrei slipped from the bottom of the vine and crashed down onto Molnar, who had been standing with his arms outstretched below. The pair collapsed against the forest floor; Andrei was shaken and bruised, but alive. Molnar shoved him off and Xavier pulled them both up to their feet. The amargasaurus were still circling the men, stamping and ululating as the deinonychus squirreled down the ficus.

"Michael," Andrei gasped, looking at Xavier. "Where's Michael?"

Xavier looked at Andrei; he shook his head, said nothing.

Syd Kinane put a wide paw on Andrei's shoulder and pointed through the pendulous legs of the orbiting Amargasaurus. Beyond the marching animals lay Michael's body; he had landed on his back, and from what Andrei could gleam, the fall had split his head open. The exposed grey-matter was being lapped up by the deinonychus that had knocked him out of the tree. A few other deinonychus were hopping through the foliage to join their kin in consuming the kill. The other deinonychus were crunching and gnawing through Craig in the ficus overlooking the nesting site.

Andrei felt hot liquids drizzling down onto the back of his head as the branches overhead were shaken. He put a hand to the sticky miasma and held his fingers before his face; slick-black crimson. A hot, jellied lump smacked the back of Andrei's head, spilling fetid waste across his shoulders as it rolled down the length of his spine. He stood there, shivering and shaking, hands held out before him.

"Shit," Andrei wheezed. "*Its shit.*"

"What do we do, Captain?" Syd called out. "I can't get a clear shot with these long-necks running around us."

Xavier walked past Syd and put an arm around Andrei's shoulders. Andrei didn't react; he only stared at the palms of his bloody shit-stained hands. Xavier knelt down, bringing Andrei to his haunches beside him. They sat in the fetid fat-saturated soil beside the amargasaurus carcass. Syd, Konnor, and Molnar kept their rifles aimed at the deinonychus beyond the spiral of sauropods.

[108]

"We wait," Xavier said. "When the deinonychus are gone, when the Amargasaurus are gone, we'll see what we can send back to Michael and Craig's families. Get the radio and call for an evac. We're going to wait this out."

A banshee's wailing cut through the fracas of amargasaurus and deinonychus. All of the dinosaurs went still from the tell-tale howl of the valley's apex predators returning home. The deinonychus in the ficus were the first animals to flee, leaping from the buzzing apiary to the safety of taller trees. The few deinonychus that were actively eating Michael's corpse attempted to drag their kill away, but they couldn't beat the utahraptors.

Nothing could beat the utahraptors.

A gargantuan dromaeosaurid wrapped in layers of leaf-like feathers sprang forth from the undergrowth and snapped its jaws around a deinonychus dragging Michael. The smaller dromaeosaurid screamed until the utahraptor severed its head with a squeeze of its jaws. The other two remaining deinonychus turned to flee, but a pair of utahraptors materialized from the shadows of the forest behind them. The trio of utahraptors quickly cornered the two deinonychus and kicked them down, pulverizing their frail bodies against the forest floor, spilling their blood like they had done to so many hapless human victims.

Xavier was rendered immobile by the appearance of the utahraptors. He was making immediate assessments; there were three, so if it were a hunting party, there could potentially be a fourth utahraptor in the vicinity. The hunting party likely belonged to Sobek Colony, which meant that there was still hope to find the rest of the flock before they could lose the trail.

The amargasaurus stood their ground defiantly between their dead kin and the utahraptor pack. The utahraptors studied the herbivores coolly with the same look

[109]

Xavier had seen from Mr. Crowley months ago. Xavier and the rest of Stalker Force kept their rifles on the utahraptors, angling the barrels between the legs of the amargasaurus family. The utahraptors grunted and growled as they edged closer.

The utahraptors began to bark and fan their forearm feathers in an attempt to scare off the sauropods. Xavier believed they were trying to claim their old nesting site, or potentially salvage what was left of the amargasaurus carcass. The amargasaurus were unperturbed by the trio of utahraptors. The sails of the amargasaurus began to flash vibrant, bloody red. The amargasaurus lowered their necks and stamped their feet. The sails bulged with the passage of air through the bioluminescent sails. The roaring of the amargasaurus was overpowering in resonance.

Xavier kept his M16 in one hand and put his other hand on Andrei's shoulder, squeezing it reassuringly. Andrei blinked a few times, focused on the scene before him, and exhaled.

"Defensive behavior," Andrei muttered.

"It's working," Xavier said.

The utahraptors turned away from the amargasaurus and trotted further into the forest. Xavier caught a dark motion blur of emerald in his periphery and jerked his head around to look. A fourth utahraptor, half-hidden amongst the undergrowth, ran past Stalker Force and the amargasaurus. Xavier recognized the thorns of ivory covering the fourth utahraptor's skull; it was Sobek, the alpha male of the last remaining utahraptor colony.

Xavier whipped the M16 back up to his cheek as Sobek swept over Michael's body.

[110]

Xavier didn't have time to pull the trigger; Sobek the utahraptor and Michael's body were both gone in a flash of movement, lost to the forests of Vietnam. The amargasaurus fell silent, swinging their tails docilely and humming in frequencies so low that the earth rippled without an audible source. Xavier lowered his rifle as he watched the sails of the amargasaurus flash tepid greens and low-lit blue.

"Time to go," Xavier said. He pulled Andrei up with one hand.

"Where," Andrei grunted bleakly. "Where…"

"Back to the evac site," Xavier said. "There's always tomorrow."

The bile began to cool on Andrei's shivering shoulders.

PRIMITIVE WARRIORS

Resplendent dawn light fell through the canopy as the sun was unsheathed from the mountain-top horizon line. The time was 0500; Stalker Force had barely spent an hour back at Jericho's base before gearing up to retrieve whatever remains could be salvaged from Michael and Craig. When the first rays of the new day needled through the black suede sky, Stalker Force and additional reinforcements returned to nesting site B.

Nguyen was sent along with Stalker Force while Mr. Crowley remained at Jericho's base. Jericho and Mr. Crowley were reaming through stacks of dossiers to find replacements for Scarecrow and Dutch, the slain Hyenas. The current Captain of Vulture Squad, a young man named Eli Taylor, had been brought in to assist with the recovery of Craig and Michael's bodies.

Xavier studied Eli Taylor in his periphery as they walked and talked through the splendid patchwork of shadow and sunlight-dappled foliage. In the year that had passed since their last mission together, Eli had grown a full handle-bar moustache that hung like cat-tails from his tobacco-stained lips. A semi-circle of half-inch scars from a utahraptor's jaws were wrapped around his exposed right tricep like an inkless tattoo. Deinonychus talon-scars were engraved on his collar bone, and a decade of scrapping had rendered his face to a poorly chiseled effigy of a Kentuckian hick.

Eli Taylor had been a member of Vulture Squad with Xavier Wise when their former Captain, Ryan Baker, was still alive. Together they had discovered the dinosaurs, rescued Andrei Wynn, and destroyed the Russian collider. Captain Ryan Baker had sacrificed himself to the Cyclops utahraptor in order for Eli, Xavier, and Nguyen to escape. While Xavier and Andrei were ordered to start the first iteration of Stalker Force, Eli had been promoted to Captain and ordained with the responsibility of restocking Vulture Squad with new recruits.

"Got any favorites yet?"

Xavier was walking with Eli on point while Stalker Force followed close behind in a diamond formation. Andrei and Nguyen remained within the center of the group. They had already circled nesting site B but found neither utahraptors nor evidence of either deceased squad-mate. Xavier managed to find the utahraptors' tracks from the night before and set forth to find the next position of Sobek Colony.

"Not yet," Eli grunted. "Every rookie's useless."

Eli Taylor was too young to have been promoted to Captain, Xavier thought. Eli was only 24 years old, but his prior experience with the Marine Force Recon during the Battle of Hue and throughout the Tet Offensive had made him a perfect candidate to pick up where Captain Baker left off. Xavier knew that Eli had struggled with alcoholism during the period of time between the Battle of Hue and the death of Ryan Baker, but had since turned sober.

"You could always recruit Nguyen," Xavier said, flipping a thumb over his shoulder. "Get him the hell away from Jericho and his Hyenas."

"Hyenas?" Eli asked, looking over his shoulder.

They both turned; Nguyen wasn't listening.

"That's what they call themselves," Xavier said. "Nguyen's call-sign is 'Panther' now."

"Jericho's got a macabre taste in animals," Eli grunted. "'Vulture Squad, scavenging the MIA and KIA from internment camps and battlefields'. Disrespectful shit. That old man needs a boot up the ass for his sick-shit sense of humor. Have you asked'm why he calls'm '*Hyenas*'?"

"Would you?" Xavier coughed, suppressing a dry laugh. "I try to keep from talking to him as little as possible. Everything's all business and reports. I don't want any kind of insight into Jericho's psyche. I'll take him at the surface level and look no further, thank you."

Eli's laughter had been reduced to a dry cackle.

"God bless ya' for keeping your humor," Eli said. "*And* your cool head. If Ryan were in your shoes right now, he'd be dreamin' of morphine and escapin' the situation. Always kept his guilt deep down in his gut until it 'came a black hole, sucking his soul inside-out. Gotta keep yer head up and keep goin' or else yer gonna turn into something less of yourself."

"Speak for yourself," Andrei grunted.

"I am," Eli said, glancing over his shoulder. "Heard it from the horse's mouth. I'd be drinking right this second if it weren't for Captain Baker. But how're you doin', doc? Still got the shakes?"

"No," Andrei said, tightening his jaw. "I've been clean for a year."

"Good," Eli said, directing his gaze through the durian trees to a clearing ahead. "So long as the Captain didn't waste any of his breath. Can't help but think he might've wasted his life, though."

"What do you mean?" Xavier said. "We'd all be dead if it weren't for him."

"Sometimes yer better off," Eli muttered. "You think Ryan died so we could be back in this valley? Isn't this the whole reason Ryan served himself up to the Cyclops, so nobody would have to follow in his footsteps?"

"A noble sacrifice," Andrei spoke up. "But you might be right."

"Woah, wait a minute," Xavier said, turning around. To the rest of the team he said, "Stalker Force, take a second to catch your breath, drink some water. We'll keep moving in five minutes."

They stopped at the edge of the durian tree-line. The nightly mists had yet to be brought to a boil by the heat of the new day, and a gentle breeze was circulating fresh air through the dry-dirt clearing. Xavier, Eli, and Andrei sat down at the base of a four-foot wide durian tree towering over a hundred feet high. Konnor and Molnar cracked open some C-ration cans of peaches overflowing with honey-thick syrup. Syd stood watch with Nguyen, their M60 and M16 sweeping over the five-fingered cassava that tangled the forest floor.

"Okay," Xavier said slowly, methodically rubbing the unruly black beard that framed his chapped and well-chewed lips. "First off, Ryan didn't die in vain. He gave his life so that we could stop the Collider and make it home without a body bag. I'm trying to keep subjectivity out of this, but it's hard. You're talking about one of my oldest friends. I don't think his life was lost for nothing."

Eli nodded, absorbing Xavier's sentiments. He took a chaw of tobacco from a tin in his pocket and stuffed it down his lower lip so that it protruded like an underbite.

"Nah," Eli chewed, spitting a stream of black saliva. "We're still here. The dinosaurs are still here. Y'all just lost two men last night, and yer sayin' that Ryan's

[115]

death wasn't in vain? I don't think Ryan would have stood for losing more men to the dinosaurs. That was the entire point of his sacrifice. It wasn't to stop the Collider; all we had to do was blow some C4 and get the hell outta the haystack. We found the needle, had it all primed to go, and he fed himself to a utahraptor."

Xavier sighed through clenched teeth. He laid his hands in his lap and wrapped them into a conjoined fist. They listened to the rest of Stalker Force clinking cans of food, Syd and Nguyen speaking in hushed tones to one another a few meters off amongst the layers of cassava vine. Birds were crying from the canopy as they ushered in the lustrous new day.

"I don't want to talk about this anymore," Xavier exhaled, shaking his head. "We can talk shit about Jericho, the Hyenas, the CIA and the Pentagon, but not Ryan-"

Xavier caught his breath. He fingered the corner of his eye.

"Not Captain Baker."

"Nor Miller," Andrei said, glancing at Eli.

"Funny, Russian," Eli said, narrowing his eyes. "Get Miller's name outta yer mouth before I unhook that cock-holster lower jaw of yer's and pull it out myself."

"*Miller?*"

Xavier and Eli looked up to see Nguyen and Syd standing before them. Nguyen's opaque eyes suddenly shone with life, swishing fluidly within their coulee sockets.

"Speakin' of the devil," Syd muttered. "We were just talking about him."

"Miller showed me-" Eli cleared his throat. "*Us* the way. He found a map to the collider and got it to us so we could destroy it. He didn't die in vain; he saved us all from Doc Wynn's doomsday dreams and got '*Panther*' here out've a Charlie camp. In't that right, *Panther*?"

"Please don't call me that," Nguyen mumbled through his black balaclava.

"Sure thing, Nguyen," Eli said with a diagonal smile. "Tell me 'bout how things're goin' with ol' G-Jericho. Y'all been taking the war to ol' Charlie Cong? Victor Charlie gettin' the one-two from the Hyenas?"

Nguyen looked away, suddenly uncomfortable.

"Take that mask off," Eli said, staring at Nguyen. "You look like Ryan."

Nguyen winced as he threaded his fingers through the balaclava; his fingers were still wrapped in bandages from when Mr. Crowley had broken them. Pain eked through his splintered phalanges as they curled around the woolen mask. Once Nguyen tucked the black mask into his pocket, he felt the full force of Eli's gaze on his scarred, young face. His pupils were the only feature on his face that gave way to the true depth of his spirit's age.

"Tell me about the Hyenas," Eli said. "Y'all enlisted? Been admitted through the military? Are the rest of y'all from Vietnam or is it mixed?"

"Mixed," Nguyen croaked. "Mr. Crowley is the Captain, he's American. They're looking at an Egyptian and an African American as our next recruits."

"Hmm," Eli hummed, looking at Xavier. "Sounds paramilitary."

[117]

"Para-military?" Nguyen asked.

"Let me ask ya somethin'," Eli said, pointing at Nguyen. "Are you part of joint-forces? Are ya in the American military or are ya in the South Vietnamese Army?"

"American," Nguyen said, nodding gently. "I'm American now."

"Really," Eli mumbled through his mouthful of chaw. "So were ya processed as an American? Y'know, got yer citizenship?"

"Citizenship?" Nguyen repeated.

"Heh," Eli spat. "You gettin' paid?"

"Cash," Nguyen said.

"Para-military," Eli said, wiping the burgundy flecks of tobacco from his swollen lower lip. "Yer not an American citizen, Nguyen. You aren't even in the military. You're a *mercenary*. A para-military operative. People in the CIA like to have loose ends that can be cut off in any situation. They taught ya not to talk, right? Not to say nothin' 'bout who yer workin' for, who yer fightin' for, none of that?"

Nguyen shook his head woefully.

"I don't know what you mean…"

"It means yer fightin' for nothin'," Eli said. "Yer just another guy with a gun. Gettin' paid to kill for nothin' but Jericho's kicks. I don't think Miller died for you to do that. I don't think he'd ever want to see you fightin' for Jericho. Guy's greasier than utahraptor spit."

[118]

"*Dah*," Andrei piped up, nodding vigorously. "Fantastic idiom, comrade."

"Who the fuck're you callin' an *idiom*?" Eli grunted, staring at Andrei."You're the idiom, *idiom*."

"I'm not an American?" Nguyen muttered, his voice wavering.

"Don't take it too bad," Eli said, waving a hand dismissively. "It's just the way these wars are fought nowadays. You'll get used to it. You'll learn."

A breeze swirled through the dirt clearing and shifted through the tree-line of durians and cassava. Xavier was about to say something, but a rancid whiff of the wind caused him to choke. He wrinkled his nose in disgust as the wind went still.

"That must be Michael," Xavier said, covering his mouth and rising to his feet. "There's something in the clearing. Everybody, get up."

The team re-grouped around Xavier and shuffled through the tree-line, their rifle-barrels daggering through the king ferns and taro plants. The arid clearing beyond was several dozen meters wide, walled in by thick-bodied durian trees and draped sheets of cassava. To the right of the clearing was a barren hill baked into a giant dirt clod by the perpetual sunlight that fell upon it from the breach in the canopy. There were several craters gouged from the center of the copper dirt clearing. In the middle of the cratered ring was a bloody and mangled uniform covering the carcass of Michael Waters.

"There's one," Xavier said. "Wonder why they left him."

"Utah's got a sense of humor," Eli chuffed. "Bet they're watchin'."

"Da," Andrei said. "They've been quite the tricksters lately."

[119]

"They're learning," Xavier said. "But there's nothing we can do to mitigate those adaptations. Let's get Michael into the bag and get him out of here. God knows we're not getting Craig out of that tree."

"Scared of heights, apache man?" Eli drawled.

"I'm not an apache," Xavier grunted. "But no. I'm more scared of the things that are up in the trees."

Eli shuddered. "Don't remind me. Keep the memories to yerself."

"Let's get this over with," Xavier said, leading the group into the clearing. They moved quickly, side-stepping the immense pits that surrounded the corpse. Upon closer inspection, Xavier noticed that the pits were actually gargantuan burrows, tunnels leading deep into the earth.

Eli snuck a peek inside of one of the tunnels and saw that it was filled with glistening white proto-feathers. He got down to his knees to get a better look at the pearlescent-plumaged animal. Xavier was standing a few feet away, struggling to keep the surging contents of his stomach from breaching through his mortar-tight lips. The other men were pacing around the tunnels, directing their rifles in every direction that the wind pushed through the walls of hanging cassava.

"Don't fall in," Molnar said, tapping the top of Eli's helmet. "Therizino's might look funny, but they don't take well to visitors in their pits."

"*Thuh-rizz-no?*" Eli drawled, lifting a judicious brow at Molnar.

Molnar pointed into the pit.

Eli turned to the pit and doubled back, nearly swallowing his tobacco.

[120]

The dinosaur inside of the burrow, a therizinosaurus, had its fore-claws criss-crossing over the mouth of the tunnel like a set of prison bars. Each claw protruding from the therizinosaurus's red-feathered forearms was over a meter long and as thick as full-grown bamboo. Eli heard the dirt shifting beneath the heavy feathered body of the therizinosaurus. The therizinosaurus clacked its claws together, creating a rhythmic clatter that mimicked clap-sticks.

"There's the warning," Molnar smiled. "Take a step back, sir."

"Goddamned lizard-birds," Eli growled, taking another step back from the pit. "Jericho should've nuked 'em all when he had the chance."

"If I had a penny for every time one of us said that…"

The humans had taken the bait.

Sobek the utahraptor was lying in wait at the top of the hill, submerged within the tangled cassava and nigh invisible to Stalker Force. The rest of his hunting party had surrounded the ring of humans from the other three corners of the sun-soaked clearing. Sobek was waiting for the hairless apes to turn their backs, to confer with one another, but there were too many. Somebody was always watching.

If Sobek were to kill them, he would need patience.

The rack of kaprosuchus teeth in Sobek's crown tingled with the warmth of the morning rays. His hunting party would normally pursue prey only at night, but after taking the innards of Michael back to his pregnant brood, Sobek led the male utahraptors back to where they had disposed of the corpse. The humans rarely ever left the dead; it was a foolish practice, and one that Sobek intended to exploit.

[121]

The thought of fresh-bleeding primate flesh caused saliva to drain down the tusks embedded in Sobek's lower jaw. The amargasaurus he had cornered and killed with his hunting party had been lost to the near-perpetual rainfall of the monsoon season. Prey was becoming more bountiful with the rejuvenation of the jungle's life sustaining greenery, but the other carnivores in the valley were pushing his kind to the brink.

The kaprosuchus and tyrannosaurs had been bad enough to compete with; now the yutyrannus and cryolophosaurus seemed to be working symbiotically to completely remove the utahraptors from the precarious ledge of their ecological niche. Every morsel of food mattered, but being the sole protectors of their colony meant that Sobek and his hunters couldn't risk losing their lives in a fight with the humans. No matter how voracious his appetite, Sobek had to remain composed and patient atop the hill.

Fortunately for Sobek, the humans had just turned their backs.

"Are you fucking kiddin' me, Xave's?" Eli snapped, spinning Xavier around by his shoulders. "You just lost two of yer men and yer walkin' us around a bunch of fucking lizard-chickens in the dirt? Those things're as big as the rex! You see those claws? Tell me those wouldn't cut any of these fuckers in half!"

"Keep your voice down," Xavier muttered, putting a hand on Eli's shoulder. "They'll hear you."

"Fuck this, fuck that, and fuck you," Eli said, shoving Xavier back. "I'm outta here; I'll be parkin' my ass under a tree until you get yer head on straight. You got yer dog tags? You good to go? You wanna *not* follow in Ryan's footsteps?"

[122]

Xavier gripped the bloodied dog tags in his fist until the name *Michael Waters* was embedded in his palm. The other men had stopped their pacing to watch Xavier and Eli's debate over the foul, shit-stained carcass. Xavier's eyes betrayed his cool demeanor; it took everything in his fortitude to keep from driving his clenched fist into Eli's mouth.

"Wise, my ass," Eli spat. "More like fuckin' Baker Plan B."

There was a scream from the hill top, and the forms of three utahraptors shifted forth from the surrounding vegetation like paintings sliding free from their canvases. The men of Stalker Force immediately shrank into a tight circle around Xavier and Eli. Their rifles barked to life, bullets cracking through the clearing and peppering the foliage where the utahraptors had once been.

The air was still; the jungle withheld its breath.

"Fuck this," Eli said, firing his Ithaca shotgun aimlessly into the forest. He pulled the butt of the rifle to his shoulder, pumped another slug into the chamber, and fired it again with a leaf-strewing *thoom*. Before he could fire another round, Xavier grabbed the barrel of the Ithaca and shoved it to the sky. The shotgun pierced the open sky, the slug flying towards the unwavering sun as the blast echoed throughout the valley.

The ground began to move beneath their feet.

There was a great roar from the craters in the clearing, and the tree-limb length forearms of a therizinosaurus emerged from one of the pits. The three-foot claws laid flat against the ground as the huge pot-bellied animal slithered out from its dusty hovel. Xavier and the others quickly ducked out of the way as the therizinosaurus rose on its stout legs, standing thirty feet high with its neck fully

[123]

extended. The ivory-coated theropod swung its claws through the air with such force that it swept the dirt of the clearing into a flurrying sandstorm.

"Double back," Xavier cried. "Get to the evac site!"

"What?" Andrei yelped.

"Get to the fuckin' chopper!" Eli screamed.

The therizinosaurus towered over the men, howling and flapping its scarlet-feathered forearms. The herbivorous theropod loomed over Stalker Force, stamping its heavy feet, kicking up plumes of gritty red soil. The other therizinosaurus were clambering out of their tunnels, barking and chortling like oversized turkeys. Xavier paused at the edge of the clearing as the rest of the team retreated to the forest.

Xavier looked to the hill-top, and immediately went still.

Sobek, the alpha utahraptor, was standing at the top of the hill across the clearing. Sobek was a terrifying visage to Xavier; the fleshy throat stripped of its mane, gouged and pitted with scars and bite marks; the crown of the skull and the bottom of the lower jaw adorned with half-buried kaprosuchus tusks. Xavier aimed his rifle at Sobek, but the utahraptor didn't seem to notice.

Sobek was studying the therizinosaurus.

"Don't shoot, comrade," Andrei whispered over Xavier's shoulder. "We have to follow him back to his nest. We can't let him get away, but we can't kill him yet, either."

Xavier briefly saw the Cyclops utahraptor in place of Sobek.

[124]

"Kill it," Eli whispered devilishly over Xavier's other shoulder. "Git that chicken-fucker."

"Only chicken-fucker here is you," Xavier growled, lowering his M16. "Get back to the helicopter. We'll find him another day, and we'll put him down with the rest of his colony."

"*Y'all* will," Eli muttered. "I'm staying the fuck outta this."

Xavier turned and ran with the others through the jungle to where their evac helicopter, nicknamed 'The Father Vulture', was waiting. Once everybody was on board, Xavier slammed the cabin door shut and dropped down beside Eli, scowling and cussing beneath his breath. Eli was tapping his boots on the floor as the Father Vulture lifted off the emerald-capped hill and flew south to Jericho's base.

Xavier chipped the dried blood from Michael's dog tag with his thumbnail.

Baker Plan B, indeed, he thought.

BABYLON

The tracks of Sobek and his hunting party led Stalker Force from the therizinosaurus family to the outskirts of long-abandoned USSR Res-Stat 2. The colossus construct had been left to rot in the eastern-central quadrant of the valley ever since General Grigory Borodin had all of the personnel involved in his dinosaur research division slaughtered. The two-story concrete block had long since been buried in curled jade locks of rhododendron that spilled in waves over the stained cement walls. Xavier Wise was surveying the moon-lit building through a pair of binoculars from the cover of a grassy knoll.

"Real spooky," Molnar whispered behind Xavier. "Ghost town."

"Russian ghosts are quiet," Konnor said, nudging Andrei. "No vodka in the after-life."

"See for yourself, comrade," Andrei growled.

"Don't worry, Dr. Wynn," Molnar whispered. "There's plenty of vodka in Soviet Hell."

Xavier motioned for silence and returned the binoculars to his brow. Res-Stat 2 sat alone between a pair of kapok trees that guarded the forested foothills from the exposed floodplains. There was a rusted steel fence surrounding the construct; a surprising change from the electric-wire-wrapped research station that Vulture Squad had saved Andrei from. The corrugated fence stood nearly twenty feet tall, interwoven with invasive ivies, with a pair of steel doors lying half-buried in the grass where the gate once stood.

"What were the Russians researching here?" Xavier asked, lowering the binoculars to look at Andrei. "Seems like this place may have been a bit more important than Res-Stat 4."

"It was," Andrei muttered. "This was the biological warfare facility."

"Biological warfare?" Syd repeated, rising above the grass.

"*Dah*," Andrei said, nodding. "Think of the Mongolians throwing black-plague casualties over the walls of the kingdoms they were attempting to invade. Take that concept, and apply it to modern technology. You can probably assume the kind of death tolls we would be dealing with in that regard."

"I was wondering where your theories of the dromaeosaurid disease came from," Xavier grunted.

"*Dah*," Andrei said, scratching his half-formed goatee. "I was hoping we could avoid coming to this place, personally. I feel it may be better off not having this on any reports we file to Jericho…"

Xavier frowned, but instead of continuing the conversation he elected to raise his M16 instead and signaled for the rest of the team to follow him. Stalker Force disembarked from the hill, cautiously jogging through the shadows of the over-arching elephant grass and through the towering gateway. The clearing was still, silent save for the insects sibilating from the kapok trees. Xavier noted that there was a large garage door in the center of the research station's front wall. The rolling garage door had been crumpled and bent half-way up into its frame. Several sets of utahraptor footprints led Xavier through the trampled grass and up to the broken garage door.

[127]

"Probably better off blowing the building," Syd mused. "See if we can pick out any raptor bones from the wreckage, call it a day."

"I would be inclined to agree for the sake of destroying the research evidence," Andrei said. "But we can't risk losing the utahraptors. We have to find their nest…if it's even here, that is."

"Wishful thinking," Konnor whispered.

Molnar snapped his fingers approvingly.

Xavier flicked on the flash-light mounted to his rifle and ducked through the garage door. The loading bay inside was filled with paint-scraped barrels, rotten crates with sprigs of ferns sprouting from their warped wood, and various pieces of loading equipment. The spacious interior was sour with the stench of rotten plant matter and mold. Xavier swept his rifle around the room as he led the rest of Stalker Force inside.

Andrei cleared his throat, suppressing a cough in his chest.

"Been here before?" Xavier asked, glancing at Andrei.

"*Dah*," Andrei said. "This is where I worked before I made the journey to Res-Stat 4."

"Think you know your way around?" Xavier asked.

"Unfortunately," Andrei mumbled.

"Lead the way," Xavier said.

"That's what I was afraid of," Andrei coughed.

Xavier aimed his rifle's light through an open door.

"Think there's living space for the utahraptors this way?"

"*Dah*," Andrei said, nodding nervously. "Plenty of it."

"Start walking," Xavier grunted.

Andrei led Stalker Force into a narrow corridor lined with moss-covered filing cabinets and doorways to dilapidated laboratories. The men angled their rifles into the rooms as they passed, skimming over the details of tossed tables, rusting laboratory equipment, and mason jars filled with the bones of dinosaur fetuses. Molnar plucked a jar from a shelf and scrubbed the black grime off of the glass with his thumbnail until he could see the skull of a hatchling tyrannosaurus rattling around inside. Molnar raised the jar for Andrei to see.

"Miscarriage?"

"A specimen," Andrei whispered. "Cracked from an egg pilfered from the Father and Mother's nest. Those were wild times, back when we were simply researching the dinosaurs and how they had impacted the ecosystem upon being reintroduced."

"*Reintroduced*," Xavier gently scoffed. "That's what you're calling it now?"

"Forgive my lack of hyperbole," Andrei grunted.

"Looks like there's another door at the end of this hallway," Xavier said, directing the light to the end of the corridor. "Molnar, Konnor, go check it out. See what you can find. Syd and I will be back in the bay watching for any intruders."

[129]

"What about me?" Andrei asked.

"Either-or," Xavier said. "Your pick."

Molnar raised the mason jar in a mock-toast to Andrei, a sloppy grin stretched across his thin lips.

"Well," Andrei said, turning on his heel. "Back to the bay, we go."

Molnar lowered the mason jar as he watched Xavier, Syd, and Andrei scurry back up the corridor and into the pitch-black garage.

"Was it something I said?" Molnar asked, looking at Konnor.

"What, something *you* said?" Konnor asked incredulously, shaking his head. "No, never."

"Never," Andrei said. "We can't talk to Jericho."

While Molnar and Konnor were investigating the facility, Xavier had switched on an electric lantern and positioned it on the loading ramp. Syd was hunkered down on one knee beside the wall, his M60 sweeping methodically over the moonlit clearing outside.

Xavier withdrew a stolen bottle of brandy from his ruck sack and sat it down gently beside the field radio. He was playing with the cork as Andrei paced circles in the periphery of the lantern's light, his boots scuffing broken glass and crackling dry leaf litter.

"Might wanna cool off," Xavier warned as he popped the cork and took a pull from the brandy. "Mmf – good stuff. We have a job to do, Andrei. You might not like it, but you're in our boat now, and that means fessing up to important intel. Even if that means putting it in Jericho's hands."

"I'll tell," Syd said over his shoulder.

"No," Andrei said, shaking his head as he shuffled in an anxious loop. "Borodin had everybody in the research division slaughtered for one reason; to keep our crimes against humanity and nature a secret. This was just one facet of the damage we had caused; luckily our research didn't have the time to come to fruition in the form of applicable weapons. Borodin was too busy with the Collider and producing anti-matter to waste any more time on our discoveries…even if they could have meant the deaths of entire populations."

Xavier choked on his mouthful of brandy, spitting up on his tiger-fatigues.

"Excuse me, Andrei?"

"If the virus had been weaponized," Andrei said slowly. "It could have been used to kill entire swathes of the human population. You could call this research station our little *Unit 731*. The dromaeosaurids seem to carry a virus that attacks the nervous systems of birds and reptiles."

"You've told me," Xavier said, wiping his mouth dry. "You never said anything about it killing *people*."

"The virus is very unstable," Andrei said, threading his fingers around his stubbled jaw. "We found that the virus can rapidly adapt to exist in other animals. Some mammals, the wild boar and some of the water buffalo in the valley, were carriers. Some populations died off in entire waves. We observed some of our own researchers succumb to the virus, but otherwise most of us were immune."

"*Jesus*, Andrei," Xavier muttered. "We have to tell Jericho."

"Never again," Andrei said, shaking his head. "You saw what his Hyenas were doing back at the Russian compound. They were looking for intel. For what ends, we may never truly know, but personally, I would expect Jericho to follow in the footsteps of his foes-turned-forebears."

"Translation?" Syd grunted from across the loading bay.

"He thinks Jericho's gonna weaponize the virus," Xavier said. He looked from the clearing outside and back to Andrei. "I understand your paranoia, Andrei. I've been around you long enough; I know you've got all kinds of conspiracies in your head. You're the only one making a conspiracy here. If you think this virus can kill people – hell, you *said* it killed people – then we have a moral obligation to tell our superior officers and get the word out before we start to see real casualties. We can't just hide everything from the Pentagon."

"Maybe," Andrei contemplated, tilting his head from left to right. "Maybe not."

"No, Andrei," Xavier said, shaking his head fervently. "I know you're more of a naturalist than a moralist, but fuckin' *no*."

"'Maybe not' what?" Syd asked, glancing at the pair from the shadows.

"Maybe if this virus were to become an international problem rather than an American one, we can have a greater chance of global mobilization against this threat," Andrei said. "The Americans, the Russians, they're two sides of the same

[132]

coin. I couldn't trust the USSR with this information, and we haven't been able to trust Jericho with anything since I signed my life away to him. Maybe we should just let the international community act this time."

"The enemy of my enemy," Syd grinned. "I get it."

"In layman's terms, *dah*," Andrei said, nodding emphatically.

Xavier anxiously twisted the cork back into the neck of the brandy bottle.

"We can talk about it later," Xavier said. "We'll go over our options. I'm afraid of what Jericho will do when he finds out you've been hiding this kind of information, but I won't tell him anything about this place so long as we tell him more about the virus."

"Remember the CIA visit?" Andrei asked, kneeling across the lantern from Xavier. "None of them will care so long as Sobek Colony is still out there in this valley. I wouldn't be surprised if they become elated with the eventual discovery of this building."

"They'll find out sooner or later," Syd mumbled. "They always do."

"Wanna tell me what that means?" Xavier said, raising an eyebrow at Syd.

They were interrupted by shouting from the open doorway of the corridor.

"Doctor Wynn," Konnor's voice echoed through the chamber. "Doctor Wynn, we're going to need you to look at something."

"Better not be another human skull," Andrei muttered, retrieving his rucksack from the floor. "I'm getting tired of Molnar's 'gifts'."

[133]

"Be grateful he's only giving you bones," Xavier said without looking up. "Instead of the usual 'souvenirs'."

"Double-speak," Andrei grumbled as he walked down the corridor. "Always double-speak with you Americans."

Xavier and Syd were silent as they listened to Andrei, Lalo, and Molnar conversing down the hallway. A gentle breeze brushed dust through the broken garage door and up the ramp, into Xavier's face. He waved aside the scratching plume and took another pull from the bottle of brandy. The gentle rise and fall of cicada whirring from the kapok canopies outside ushered a semblance of peace within the cavernous research station. Xavier corked the brandy and placed it back in his ruck-sack, lifting his M16 in its place.

"Long days," Syd muttered softly.

"Long nights," Xavier said, shaking his head. "Makes for a hell of a longer life."

"You think so?"

"I know so," Xavier exhaled. "The sleepless nights make the weeks drag by. I just keep thinking of Craig and Michael. What I'm going to write to their families, if anything. I know I should, but what can I say? *'These things happen'*? *'Your son died in a friendly-fire accident'*? *'Dinosaurs ate your kid'*?"

"I would stick with the first one," Syd said. "Sums it up nice."

Xavier mulled this over as he listened to the gradual fade-out of the cicada songs. The floodplains were silent and still beneath the watchful eye of the moon, the waves of elephant grass shifting from black to crisp luminescent blue like an arctic

[134]

sea. Xavier looked to Syd, whom still had his M60 drifting from left to right and back again. Xavier motioned for Syd to come closer, nodding towards the clearing beyond the garage door.

Syd sniffed the air.

"I don't smell utah's…"

Xavier motioned for silence with a brisk flick of his hand.

The kapoks audibly swayed, their luscious canopies crackling.

"It's not a raptor," Xavier whispered. He placed his palm flat against the cement floor and felt a gentle trickling of vibrations ripple through his phalanges. "Not the Father T. rex, either, unless he's far off. Could be a triceratops or a parasaurolophus. We're pretty close to their territory."

"Or a kapro," Syd muttered. "Maybe a rogue male."

Crack.

Xavier flinched at the sound of metal folding inward. He rose to his feet and looked around with his rifle at the scattered silhouettes of barrels and crates. Xavier scanned the room with his light until he discovered a second garage door on the far-left side of the bay. The door had been covered with a sheet of moss and mildew, but was now noticeable due to its near ninety-degree crease in the middle. Little fluff-piles of dry moss littered the concrete floor beneath the bent door.

Xavier narrowed his eyes as the beam of light fell upon a muddy footprint.

"We're not alone in here," he whispered.

Xavier sank back from the shadows that swelled within the corners of the expansive labyrinth of equipment and cargo. The M16 fell to Xavier's waist-side as he back-pedaled into the vicinity of the lantern. Syd remained silent from his position along the wall. There was the sound of padded footsteps, talons scraping softly across the dusty concrete floor. A crate tumbled to the floor from its precarious perch atop a stack of others, and Xavier swung his rifle up in preparation to fire.

"Behind you," Syd whispered.

Xavier pivoted on his heel and aimed his M16 outside. He knelt down to look under the door and saw the lone silhouette of a theropod standing in the center of the clearing. It was built like a tyrannosaurus rex, but only three quarters of the Father T.rex's size. The dinosaur's arms were longer, muscular, and its entire body was covered in a thick coat of fur-like protofeathers.

As the yutyrannus meandered around the clearing, ducking its pale snout to investigate the footprints in the soil, its protofeathers shifted from black to a blur of green based on how the moonlight and shadows played across its body. Xavier swallowed roughly, his throat rubbing raw from the fresh coat of brandy.

"Yutyrannus," Xavier whispered in a coarse voice.

"Sir," Syd hissed.

Xavier looked over his shoulder and nearly dropped his rifle in shock. A ghastly white snout speckled with black ornamental scales began to shift through the shadows and into the light of the lone lantern. The body of the yutyrannus was nearly imperceptible in the darkness; it was as if the animal was fully materializing into reality with each steady step it took into the dim white lantern light. The yutyrannus

[136]

lowered its head to Xavier's eye-level as it sauntered towards him, its arms hanging loose, the taloned fore-claws twitching with anticipation.

Xavier aimed his M16 between the yutyrannus's scarlet brow-horns.

The yutyrannus stared at Xavier with eyes like fresh gunshot wounds.

Syd remained silent.

BABYLON II

Darkness engulfed Research Station 2.

The main laboratory was at the end of thc corridor leading from the loading bay. The expansive chamber was an amalgamation of a library, museum, and militarized office space. Shelves loaded with books, specimen jars, dinosaur bones, and various pots overflowing with ornamental plants lined the walls of the room. There was a pair of barred sky-lights in the middle of the ceiling, spilling canopy-sieved moonlight and shadows upon a lone ring of mud in the center of the filthy floor. The rotting carcass of Michael Waters was crumpled in the center of the shoddily assembled utahraptor nest.

The trap had been set.

Sobek, the alpha utahraptor with a crown of kaprosuchus tusks, was crouched within a closet facing the corridor to the loading bay from across the room. His shaggy coat stirred as he coiled back on his legs, preparing for the right moment to pounce upon the hairless apes of Stalker Force.

Sobek had left one of his hunting party pack-mates with the beta males and females back at their nesting site while the other two hunters were off searching the lowland hills for stygimoloch and other small animals to bring to the colony. Sobek had brought Michael's carcass into the research station to set up another ambush, and it was almost time for him to strike.

Sobek stretched his taloned fore-fingers, allowing the muscles to slacken and constrict with each flexion. The three-inch claws were dark and scuffed, incapable of capturing the moonlight that seeped into the room. He had his eyes resting on the smallest of the three humans, the disheveled young scientist kneeling before the make-shift nest. The scrawny primate was flanked by two larger, more heavily armed pack-mates.

Sobek could visualize his course of action as if it were a preconceived memory. He imagined himself leaping from the shadows, plunging his foot-long toe claws through Andrei's stomach while simultaneously taking the other two primates to the ground with his forelimbs. Once the three were on the ground, Sobek would dispatch each of them methodically, taking his time to savor the taste of their flesh. Sobek was a clever utahraptor, surviving by tenacious instinct and cunning prescience. He fully understood the rifle-wielding mammals were a threat to the existence of his brood. If Sobek's kind were to survive, it would require spilling the blood of each and every ape plaguing the valley.

Sobek drooled as he remembered the taste of human intestines.

"This nest is all wrong, comrade."

"What are you talking about?" Molnar asked, motioning to the wide ring of frond-littered mud. "It's even got egg shells in it. Hell, Michael's in it. I don't know what else you need to face facts; we found it."

"Nah," Andrei said, flicking aside the shell fragments from Michael's carcass. "We're tracking a colony, not a singular family. Just based off of the shell fragments in this nest, this would belong to a utahraptor family with incredibly low clutch yields. There's always the chance we got led to this abandoned nest for a reason…"

"Let me guess; another trap?" Konnor sighed with exaggerated exasperation. "Come on, we have to be better than this."

[139]

"I'm willing to accept everything within the realm of possibility," Andrei said, crushing a shell in his fist as he rose from the nest. "Unfortunately, it seems like these utahraptors are stretching the parameters of possibility. We should get back to Xavier and Syd so we can call in an evac. I don't think we're going to find our colony tonight; if we're lucky…"

A deep, rumbling purr shook the specimen jars and potted plants adorning the shelves along the walls. Andrei, Molnar, and Konnor looked to one another as a kaprosuchus skull clattered to the floor from its high perch.

Sobek inhaled sharply through his nostrils; an unintentional reaction upon recognizing the vocalizations of his colony's deadliest threat. The humans looked towards the source of Sobek's noise, but he was nestled too deep within the darkness of the closet to be seen. Andrei was looking from the closet to the rumbling corridor when Konnor took him by the arm.

"Come on," Konnor said, pulling Andrei to the hall. "We need to look."

"Yutyrannus," Andrei exhaled shakily. "It has to be."

Sobek was growing restless. The humans were half-way to the door; in a few seconds they would be out of his reach and on their way out. Sobek trembled slightly, suddenly unsure of what to do. If the other humans were in the building, they could potentially halt his ambush, or even worse; kill the remaining bastion of his fledgling colony. He needed to act before his only opportunity was lost.

"Let's hope they're outside," Konnor said. "We can't afford-"

Andrei heard the rush of feathers gusting through the silent space, the wet plunge of talons tearing through abdominal tissue, and he was thrown to the floor. Andrei started crawling without thinking, clambering to his feet beside Molnar as

[140]

Sobek screeched from behind. Konnor screamed from the shadows as the utahraptor's fore-claws cleaved heavily through his sternum.

Andrei covered his ears as Molnar's shotgun fired over his head. Andrei attempted to decipher Molnar's abject screaming through the ringing in his ears. He saw Konnor flailing beneath Sobek with each flash of the shotgun's muzzle flare, illuminating the ribs that had been slashed open, the exposed lungs pumping dark fluids in the bony cavern of his chest.

Sobek shook Konnor's lungs ravenously before swallowing.

Andrei was wrenched off of his feet by Molnar and dragged towards the corridor. It took a few seconds for Andrei to mentally force his legs to carry his own weight. Molnar shoved Andrei down the hall and rotated on his heel, redirecting his remington to the sounds of mutilation in the main laboratory.

Molnar saw the moonlight falling upon the mangled and twitching carcass of Konnor, but Sobek was gone. Molnar back-pedaled down the hall-way to the loading bay, where Andrei was crouched by the door. Andrei waved Molnar back, putting a finger before his own trembling lips. Molnar was about to voice his confusion when he heard the sudden vibrato of a yowling yutyrannus.

The great white snout of a yutyrannus drifted by the doorway. The theropod's scarlet eyes leered down the hallway from its blanched sockets. The yutyrannus attempted to force its body into the corridor, huffing and groaning as its red-sheathed horns scraped the door-frame. Andrei ducked away from the yutyrannus's swinging head and scrambled over to Molnar's side.

Sobek was watching Andrei and Molnar from the shadows of the laboratory. He couldn't keep still; he had half of the human pack cornered against a

[141]

hungry yutyrannus. This was his only chance to slaughter the trapped apes, but one had a shotgun and was capable of killing Sobek. The yutyrannus was a greater threat than Sobek cared to risk facing. Sobek knew he had to take his opportunity before it was lost.

"Get back," Molnar barked to Andrei.

Molnar fired the remington down the corridor as Sobek blurred from one pitch-black corner of the laboratory to the other. Molnar started backpedaling again, but Andrei was hollering about the yutyrannus that was half-way inside of the hall-way. Molnar turned and saw the yutyrannus dragging itself inside, clawing at the floor with its thick fore-fingers. The yutyrannus swung its head to the side, puncturing the cement walls with its brow-horns. Molnar stared helplessly as the yutyrannus's fore-claws carved screeching lines through the concrete floor.

"We're trapped," Andrei cried. "Good as dead!"

"Just you," Molnar barked over his shoulder. "I'm gettin' outta here alive."

Molnar heard the rush of Sobek's feathers and threw himself on top of Andrei. Andrei's head ricocheted off of the cement with the sharp *crack* of a fresh fracture. Molnar heaved himself over Andrei's immobile figure as Sobek sailed overhead. The utahraptor's killing toe-talons were aimed forward, his long arms outstretched with hooked claws splayed. Sobek screeched as he flew straight over the hairless apes and directly onto the yutyrannus wedged in the doorway.

The impact was instantly heard throughout the research station.

Sobek screamed desperately, flailing his shaggy forearms as the yutyrannus bellowed ferociously, slamming its tail against the floor of the loading bay. Molnar clamped his hands over his ears to keep from going deaf. He raised his head an inch

[142]

and saw Sobek being thrown against the floor in the yutyrannus's jaws. The yutyrannus slammed the utahraptor repeatedly against the concrete floor, each impact resonating with the crackling of splintering bones.

Molnar winced and lowered his eyes.

He almost felt sorry for Sobek.

"*Now*," Xavier hissed. "*Do it.*"

Xavier and Syd were pressed against the wall of the loading bay as the second yutyrannus scraped its talons along the crumpled garage door. The theropod was gently probing its way into the musty room, taking its time to keep from making too much noise. When the yutyrannus trapped in the doorway began to bellow and roar with rage, the second yutyrannus quickly turned agitated.

The yutyrannus stuck its head under the garage door and bent it completely upward with an upward thrust of its snout. The metal creaked as it crumpled against the tyrannosaurid's blood-red muzzle.

"*Now*," Xavier barked.

Xavier fired his M16 at the back legs of the yutyrannus wrestling with Sobek while Syd fed a belt through his M60 and opened fire on the yutyrannus entering the chamber. The yutyrannus trapped in the corridor began to bark and whimper in distress, stamping its heavy feet in frustration as it attempted to back its way out of the narrow corridor. Syd kept firing upon the second yutyrannus, forcing

[143]

it back outside by chewing through its iridescent mane with heavy automatic firepower.

The yutyrannus in the doorway finally backed out of the corridor and into the loading bay, toppling several stacks of crates and barrels that went clattering and clanging across the floor. Xavier feigned away from a rolling oil drum as the yutyrannus stumbled around the garage, Sobek clinging to its side. Sobek had his foot talons embedded in the flank of the yutyrannus, and his forearms were clinging to its sleek-feathered spine. Xavier's jaw slid loose when he saw the wily old alpha utahraptor with the crown of tusks riding the thrashing titan.

"*Run,*" Andrei screamed.

Xavier turned just as Molnar and Andrei came sprinting past, bee-lining straight to the loading bay door. The yutyrannus outside of the garage came barreling forward with its head held low, swinging its horns and ridged muzzle through the crumpled door. The twisted metal went sailing through the air and struck the other yutyrannus fighting with Sobek on the side of its head.

The yutyrannus swung its head around, snapping its jaws as the bent roll of sheet metal clanged against the floor. Sobek attempted to climb onto the yutyrannus's back to force the animal to the floor, but the second yutyrannus charged towards him, its jaws poised to take a chunk from Sobek's spine.

Sobek retracted his talons from the yutyrannus's feathered coat and kicked off from the theropod, flinging himself across the room. Sobek crashed into a tower of crates as the two yutyrannus collided and fell against the back wall of the loading bay.

[144]

Sobek immediately climbed to his feet, trembling on listless legs, his rib cage bent and bruised beneath lacerated torso tissue. He saw the two yutyrannus snapping at one another, quarreling, and quickly directed his attention back to the fleeing primates. He saw the bearded alpha male of the pack, Xavier, waving the rest of the survivors outside.

Sobek caught Xavier by his eyes and spread his plucked forearms, screaming voraciously through broken fangs and flowing blood. Sobek coiled back to pounce, but a well-placed shot from Xavier's M16 caught the utahraptor in the shoulder. Sobek stumbled back with the force of the shot, rearing back as blood drained from the fresh wound.

Sobek looked up from his injury and saw that the yutyrannus had finished their quarreling. The larger theropods were redirecting their bloody pupils towards Sobek's beaten body. The old alpha utahraptor looked back to the humans, already charging across the clearing to the foothills beyond the perimeter fence. Taking the rest of the survivors down would be too risky; they were back in their pack, and they had their eyes on Sobek and the research station. Sobek knew he would have to continue the hunt another day, or else he would risk dooming his Colony with his own pointless martyrdom.

Sobek shrieked as he leapt away from a charging yutyrannus. The 30-foot long tyrannosaurid collided head-first with a concrete wall, shaking the building's support beams. Sobek turned away from the pair of yutyrannus and stumbled out of the loading bay, sprinting as fast as his legs could carry him back into the depths of the jungle.

Sobek would deal with the yutyrannus first; the humans would die next.

"Konnor's gone," Molnar declared, heaving his rucksack into the elephant grass. He spun around and aimed his remington at the research station, but the old alpha Sobek was already gone. There was a blur of green blending through the shadows, then nothing. Sobek was immediately lost to the expansive mountain range.

"*Goddammit*," Xavier growled, dropping down beside Molnar's rucksack. He put his hands over his face and rubbed his eyes vigorously, working his palms through his cheeks. "Jesus Christ, not again. Not so soon. It hasn't even been a week since..."

"They're still roaring and carrying on," Syd mused, laying a hefty paw on Xavier's shoulder. "Maybe they got the alpha raptor."

"They didn't," Molnar grunted. "He got away."

Xavier punched Molnar's rucksack, forcing the air from it.

"Fucking *utah's*," Xavier hissed through his teeth. Beneath his breath, in an airy whisper, he said, "*This can't keep happening. Keep cool, Xaves. Keep cool. Think of Logan. Think of Ryan. Can't keep doing this. Can't keep doing this...*"

Molnar knelt down across from Xavier in the dewy grass.

"There's always a silver lining, boss," Molnar said. "Just watch."

Molnar withdrew a small remote from his pocket and played with its switch. Xavier raised his eyes to watch Molnar, and Andrei looked up as well. The men were silent as they listened to Molnar rapidly click the remote. The yutyrannus were still howling and bellowing further downhill. The screams of Sobek's colony began to rise from the mountain walls like the nocturnal mist.

[146]

"Molnar," Xavier said slowly. "What are you…"

"Just wait," Molnar said, motioning for silence with a raised hand.

Click click click.

"The range isn't too good on these," Molnar admitted.

"Molnar…"

The roaring of the yutyrannus reached a pitch of ear-ringing clarity as the theropods charged out of the research station, their tails waving behind them. The silhouetted predators stomped around the clearing, growling and groaning from deep within their throats, their snouts darting to and fro. The yutyrannus raised their heads to examine the source of the clicking sound coming from the hills beyond the research station's fence.

One of the yutyrannus, the male that had suffered some lacerations from Sobek, fixed its glowering red eyes onto Molnar and hissed through its teeth. The sound made Xavier shudder.

"Molnar-" Andrei warned.

The research station suddenly erupted. A mushroom cloud of fire bloomed through the decimated ceiling and rose high enough to scorch the canopies of the hundred-foot-high kapok trees. The walls of the research station fell forward, crashing at the feet of the startled yutyrannus. The rusted fences laid flat to the earth as smoke rolled through the foot-hills, sieving through the elephant grass. The pair of yutyrannus started running from the raging inferno, barking and yelping until they vanished from sight and sound within the jungle. Xavier stared at the roiling flames as Molnar golf-clapped with his back turned.

[147]

"I was hoping it'd take the yuty's out too," Molnar said. "But what can you do. The tax-man's always cutting corners when it comes to budgeting explosive ordinance. Call it a Sin Tax."

"What the hell did you *do*?" Syd wheezed, a hand over his heart.

"Found some barrels of diesel," Molnar shrugged. "Strapped down some C4, *click-click*, *bang-boom*, we've got our asses covered and Andrei's got his little viral wish fulfilled."

"Who the hell gave *you* C4?" Xavier exclaimed, tearing his hands from his soot-stained face to stare dumbfounded at Molnar.

"Nobody gives me shit; you know that," Molnar said. "Can't even get a butter knife in the commissary. I had to take that C4, Captain. You never know when it could come in handy…like tonight. It got the yuty's and Sobek far from us. It got the dangerous bio-weapon intel from falling straight into the hands of Jericho's bureaucrats."

"But Konnor…" Xavier trailed off, shaking his head solemnly.

Molnar smiled as he squeezed Xavier's shoulder.

"Believe me," Molnar said with a distant smile. "Some things are better left buried."

"What happened to Konnor," Xavier asked with weak desperation, looking from Molnar to Andrei. "What happened?"

Andrei thought of Sobek, the shadows, the screams. He started to shake.

"Better left buried, comrade."

[148]

FREE BIRD

The dry season had finally taken hold of the valley.

From the fountainhead waterfall at the conjoined crown of the mountain walls, all the way to the sun-saturated emerald floodplains that rose from the drying delta, the cleansing rays of the sun were felt. At the southern-most end of the valley where the quarantine walls stood in defiance of herbivorous dinosaur herds in search of water, Captain Xavier Wise and the men of Stalker Force were performing one of many routine round-ups.

Xavier Wise was riding in the passenger seat of an olive-drab Jeep galloping across the floodplains. Because of the dry season, much of the delta where the river spread out from the end of the valley had become fertile ground beneath the padded feet of the azure-scuted triceratops and thirty-foot long parasaurolophus.

The parasaurolophus were covered in lime-green leather akin to the creased and wrinkled hides of elephants. Magenta-rimmed scarlet tubercles adorned the splotchy coats of the male parasaurolophus, while the females were painted in drab olive tones with charcoal-colored spinal ridges. The herd of parasaurolophus moved as one wholly functioning body, never parting ways except to make room for the triceratops and countless stygimoloch.

Xavier watched the herd of parasaurolophus through the lens of his binoculars. It was difficult for Xavier to make out just how many of the animals there were, as they had been spooked into a congealed mass by the circling jeeps. With all of their bodies pressed together, the parasaurolophus appeared as a shifting conglomeration of fiery red spots swimming through swampy greens, creating an illusory and nauseating effect. Xavier had to pull the binoculars away to keep from

[149]

getting sick. The roll bars rattling around his head with each bounce of the jeep's shocks didn't help his swelling migraine.

"Syd, slow down," Xavier said, pulling his head back from the wind blasting through the mesh-screened window. "We need to chase them away from the perimeter, not race 'em."

Syd pumped the brakes and the Jeep skidded across the soggy turf of the delta. The soil was loose and soupy beneath the vehicle's tires. The Jeep churned mud as Syd changed gears.

It was easy for Xavier to tell where the tributaries had been drained from the delta. Where the water once ran through, there were gaps in the perimeter wall that had been webbed across with a patch-work of razor-wire.

The triceratops and parasaurolophus would easily tear their way through the razor wire unless Stalker Force diverted the herds. The Army Corps of Engineers were on stand-by a safe distance beyond the concrete-and-razor wire perimeter. As soon as the herds were redirected further into the valley, the final construction of a dam could commence.

With the perimeter wall rushing past his mesh-screened window, Xavier turned to the left and craned his neck to see past Syd. When he rose to his feet, half-way kneeling on the seat, Xavier was able to poke his head above the roll-bars of the jeep and see across the floodplain. The wind played with his beard and onyx mane as he raised a hand to block the incessant rays of the mid-day sun.

The parasaurolophus were parting from their tightly-knit group to thread their way through the triceratops. The male parasaurolophus possessed red-rimmed duck-bills coated in translucent keratinous sheaths. Long, membranous crests were

[150]

supported from the base of their necks to the tip of a phallic backwards-facing bone that jutted from their craniums. When the parasaurolophus spotted the jeep, they tilted their heads forward so their crests would stand tall, bruised black and bloody red, the sunlight shining through.

Syd laid on the horn, and the parasaurolophus returned a near-perfect imitation of the sound. Xavier laughed in surprise as Syd suddenly jerked the wheel to the right, feigning away from the herbivores. A few of the parasaurolophus uttered a resonant, whirring buzz from their opened beaks akin to the songs of cicada that filled the night air. Xavier fought to hide his smile as he watched the parasaurolophus amble away from the fence.

"They're no doubt looking for water," Xavier said, his voice carried off by the rushing wind. "I've never seen animals so large able to make noises like that. It's almost like a mockingbird, or a parrot."

"It's not so surprising," Andrei called from the back of the Jeep. He was holding a roll bar in one hand and clutching his seat belt tight in the other. "These animals are ancestors of birds. They had millions of years to evolve; who's to say what kind of adaptations can occur in that span of time?"

"Hell if I know," Xavier said, lowering his voice. "Geek."

"I heard that," Andrei snapped.

Molnar laughed from beside Andrei. The other jeep that was circling the parasaurolophus opposite of Xavier's jeep held Grant Robelle and Alan Malcolm, Stalker Force's newest sniper-spotter team, as well as Lalo Florez, their new medic at the wheel.

[151]

The jeep that Lalo was steering sped up, taking a tight turn around the rear-right flank of the parasaurolophus herd. The tail-end of the vehicle struggled to find solid ground and fish-tailed wildly to the left as Lalo fought with the clutch. The tires gripped soil and spat mud in a high arc as the vehicle launched itself forward. One of the parasaurolophus, venturing too close to the jeep, danced backwards on its stout legs as the vehicle revved past. The parasaurolophus mimicked the rising groan of the Jeep's engine as Lalo sped away, whooping and hollering at the wheel.

The triceratops weren't as frightened of the jeeps as the parasaurolophus. Despite being roughly the same size and fully capable of sending the jeeps rolling like tin cans in the wind, the parasaurolophus were more skittish and easy to steer and scare. The triceratops, however, swung their heads at the jeeps if they sped by too close. Molnar sat in the back seat with his remington filled with bird-shot; incapable of hurting the triceratops, but perfectly suited for annoying them.

Molnar howled as he wriggled his body through the roll-bars and took aim at the meandering triceratops herd. The bull triceratops that helmed the herd was an ancient leviathan, replete with scars that told wordless stories of bloodshed across his body. The alpha male moved through his herd without fear, holding his head high as he trotted past on swift, stocky legs. If the Bull decided to take a quarrel to Stalker Force, it would be up to Syd and Lalo to get them out alive. A single impact from the Bull would be enough to crumple the jeeps like a mortar shell.

"Remember," Andrei howled through the wind. "Aim for their frills, not their faces! We're pissing them off, not blinding them!"

"Bull can't kill us if he can't see," Molnar barked, lining the barrel of his shotgun up with the face of a nearby triceratops. "I'm a good shot."

"Eye for an eye," Xavier shouted. "Don't let those trikes hit us blind!"

Molnar fired the shotgun, peppering a triceratops's face with miniscule flak. The bullets barely scraped through the skin that covered the animal's frill, but it was enough to draw blood and an irritated groan from the hefty ceratopsid. The triceratops turned away, and the jeep had to swerve to avoid its swinging tail. Molnar hugged the roll-bars as the animal's tail brushed against his back.

Molnar was nearly dislodged, but he held tight and aimed the shotgun back at the herd. The rest of the triceratops were already making their way further inland, following the parasaurolophus back to the forested hills.

"Too easy," Molnar shouted. "One shot and they run."

"Like shooting fish in a barrel," Syd hollered.

"More like trap-shooting," Molnar grinned. He fired another round of buckshot at the hind-quarters of a triceratops, fraying the quills from its back. The dinosaur grunted in alarm like a startled boar and staggered forward, barreling after its herd-mates to the main artery of the river. The herd appeared to stop their journey half-way across the floodplain. Molnar stared as the herds began to turn back towards the perimeter wall.

"Why are they coming back?" Syd shouted.

A thunderous roar sent hundreds of birds flying from the canopy.

"You get three guesses," Molnar yelled. "First two don't count!"

"The Father," Xavier yelled. "Inciting a stampede!"

The triceratops were the first ones barreling forward. They were charging straight towards the jeeps with their heads held low, towards the razor-wire patches in the perimeter wall. Xavier was surveying the situation through his binoculars when he saw the predators that were chasing the parasaurolophus and triceratops. There were four large theropods, half the size of the Father T. rex, each covered in a thin coat of shimmering amber proto-feathers. Fluid black stripes, like running mascara, were visible through the carnivores' silken feathers.

"Cryolophosaurus," Andrei shouted. "Keep your distance!"

"Brilliant strategy," Syd grunted as he steered the jeep. "Really, doc. Brilliant."

Each of the cryolophosaurus were roughly 25 feet long, standing 9 feet high and at the peak of sexual maturity. The sexual dimorphism between the predators was visible through their crests; the three males had forked crests of iridescent blue and black protofeathers rising from bony plates atop their skulls. Only one of the cryolophosaurus was female; the matriarch of the hunting posse. Her bony crest was bare of feathers from head-butting other females in contests for supremacy of her beta male harem.

The much more robust and battle-scarred Matriarch dwarfed her lithe male counterparts. She was nearly 28 feet long and a thousand pounds heavier than her betas. The triceratops were much larger and more powerfully built than the four-strong party of cryolophosaurus, but the predators were working in tandem to chase the stragglers at the back of the herd. Natural selection in the form of a bloody stampede; the weak and elderly parasaurolophus and triceratops were quickly trampled and left for the cryolophosaurus to finish off.

"Big boy's mad," Molnar shouted, pointing across the floodplain.

"*Shit*," Xavier barked. "Here they come!"

[154]

As the Bull triceratops charged the cryolophosaurus Matriarch, the herd of stampeding parasaurolophus and triceratops trampled around the jeeps. Lalo and Syd fought with the wheels of their jeeps, causing the vehicles to swerve wildly around the leathered and armored bodies. They were lost in a sea of titans; it was impossible for any of the men to see over the backs of the confused dinosaurs around them. Syd spat and swore as he followed Lalo's jeep through the calamity.

"They're circling," Andrei shouted. "We have to get out or we'll be crushed!"

"*Great observation*," Syd snapped.

Molnar aimed his remington at the sky and fired slug after slug of birdshot into the air. The report of the shotgun was deafening when surrounded by the scaly bodies of the dinosaurs. Xavier dropped his binoculars and clapped his hands over his ears. It was bad enough that the dinosaurs were howling and roaring in decibels unwelcoming to human ears without Molnar adding to his tinnitus.

The report from the shotgun caused the herd to part from the vehicles. Lalo's jeep lunged out of the herd first, followed by Syd's jeep. When the vehicles climbed out from the splashing pit, the sun shone fully through the roll bars and windshield. The men inside of the jeeps listened as the wind whistled through their ears, and the roaring of the herds gave way to the howling of two titans in a brutal clash.

Across the clearing, the Bull triceratops was circling the Matriarch cryolophosaurus. The Matriarch was backed up by her posse of pea-cocking beta males. The theropods moved with the graceful fluidity of herons through the ankle-high water. The Bull lowered his head to the Matriarch as he eyed her male harem. The old Bull understood what it meant to get flanked by predators; battling sub adult

[155]

tyrannosaurs during the late Cretaceous had taught him a wealth of knowledge in predator behavior.

One of the beta cryolophosaurus broke formation and charged to the flank of the Bull triceratops. The Bull swung his head sharply to the left, catching the forelimbs of the cryolophosaurus between his jagged horns. With a twist of his head, the Bull shattered the bones in the predator's forearm and threw the shrieking carnivore to the ground.

Before the cryolophosaurus could right itself, the Bull coiled back on his hind-legs and propelled himself forward. The cryolophosaurus had mere seconds to scream before the Bull's fore-feet crushed the predator's head beneath the marshy turf. The crunch of the cryolophosaurus' skull audibly marked one less predator for the Bull to deal with.

"Bad move," Xavier said.

The jeeps had stopped their circling. The herds were no longer stampeding; the herbivores had stopped short of the fence and were turning back to watch the primitive combat. Several triceratops and parasaurolophus stood within mere meters of the jeeps as they collectively watched the bloody brawl. While the Bull had his back turned, the Matriarch leapt forward and buried her claws into his quilled back. She attempted to get a bite out of the Bull's hump-back, but the razor-sharp keratinous filaments quickly rebuked her efforts.

"She's coming back!" Molnar shouted, pointing.

A parasaurolophus turned to face Molnar inquisitively.

"Not you," Molnar said, waving away the herbivore dismissively. "She's never coming back, Johnny."

"Why do we bring this guy along?" Syd asked, jabbing a thumb back at Molnar.

"I've been asking myself the same thing," Xavier sighed.

"*Run*," Molnar shouted across the floodplain, slapping the frame of the jeep. "Run, big boy!"

The Bull glanced over his shoulder at Molnar just as the Matriarch lunged for his throat. The Matriarch's teeth buried into the flesh of the Bull's neck, but he jerked his head away and cracked his bony frill against the Matriarch's head. The Matriarch yowled and raked her claws at the Bull's hide, but the lacerations barely sank lower than an inch through his thick osteoderms. Before the Matriarch could take another swipe at his throat, the Bull reared back on his hind-legs, toppling her aside.

"My bad," Molnar shouted, waving at the Bull.

"Quit it," Xavier said, slapping Molnar's helmet. "Let him do his thing."

"Bubba's got bigger things to worry about," Molnar said. "Look!"

The two surviving beta male cryolophosaurus sprang across the clearing and tackled into the side of the Bull triceratops. The Bull staggered, teetering on his hind-legs, and landed powerfully onto his side. The triceratops's impact caused the earth to rumble beneath the jeeps. The Matriarch seized the moment and charged for the Bull's neck, bounding across the clearing with her fanged jaws angled at the triceratops's bulging throat wattle.

The sudden roar of the Father T. rex blasted through the floodplains.

[157]

Andrei leapt a foot in the back of the jeep.

The men of Stalker Force looked around; the Father T. rex was nowhere to be seen. The parasaurolophus that Molnar had called 'Johnny' was watching Molnar expectantly, as if anticipating a response. Molnar looked at the curious herbivore and gesticulated at it, throwing his arms to scare the animal off.

"Go on, git," Molnar shouted. "Don't you hear that rex?"

"Unless…" Andrei muttered, rubbing his jaw. "Maybe he is our T. rex."

"What do you mean?" Syd asked.

The parasaurolophus tilted its head back and released a booming roar that near-perfectly mimicked the vocalization of the Father T. rex. It was slightly higher in pitch, but if heard from across the valley, it could have easily passed for a full grown Tyrannosaur. The triceratops had taken notice and were pacing restlessly, but the other parasaurolophus in the herd understood what was happening. They were engaging in an ancient form of psychological warfare; mimicry.

The beta male cryolophosaurus backed away from the Bull in their panic. The amber-bodied theropods moved around the clearing frantically, their heads bobbing left and right as they attempted to spot the roaring tyrannosaurus rex. The parasaurolophus herd in its entirety joined in the illusion, creating a chorus of thunderous howls that seemed to the cryolophosaurus as a warning from a family of hungry adult tyrannosaurs.

The beta male cryolophosaurus abandoned their Matriarch to flee.

"No girl's worth dying over," Molnar muttered. "Not here."

[158]

The Matriarch cryolophosaurus dismounted the Bull triceratops' back and turned to howl after her fleeing stags. While the Matriarch was distracted, the Bull triceratops heaved himself upright to his feet. The Bull's breathing was labored by his broken ribs, but he was capable of holding his own weight. The Matriarch was too busy bellowing at her cowardly betas to take notice of the Bull triceratops.

"Oh, shit!" Andrei shouted.

The Matriarch turned just as the Bull crashed head-first into her torso. The Bull's horns punched up through the cryolophosaurus's abdomen and burst through the row of ornamental spines that lined her back. The Bull lifted his head and leaned back on his hind legs, raising the Matriarch high into the air above him. The Matriarch slid down the length of the triceratops's horns, wailing and kicking her shaggy hind-legs in feeble agony. The Bull touched his beaked snout to the earth and the Matriarch slid free from his brow-horns, splashing heavily before him.

The Matriarch struck the marsh floor with the force of a falling car. The jeeps bounced on their shocks, and the men stared in silence as the Bull triceratops circled his dying victim. The beta-male cryolophosaurus were watching from the periphery of the forests that lined the floodplains, but when they saw their Matriarch bleeding out, they simply turned tail and headed back into the safety of the jungle. The Matriarch could only mewl and drag herself away from the Bull as the victor approached his victim.

"What's he doing?" Syd asked. "Why doesn't he finish her off?"

"To supplement his diet," Andrei said. He was staring patiently from over Molnar's shoulder. They listened as the dying cryolophosaurus yowled helplessly. "The triceratops are omnivorous. Iron and Protein are important for their diet."

[159]

The Bull triceratops clamped his beaked jaws around the cryolophosaurus's neck. The triceratops's beak, sharpened to a dagger-edge by decades of feasting on roots, easily carved a clean hunk of flesh from the Matriarch's throat. The dying Matriarch's cries fell to withering chokes that quickly fell flat beneath the gurgling babble of flowing blood.

The Bull faced the herds of triceratops and parasaurolophus as he lazily chewed his mouthful of cryolophosaurus. When the Bull noticed the other herbivorous dinosaurs staring, he spread his long jaws open and howled, spraying a fine red mist through his crimson-stained beaks.

"Pretty inspiring spectacle," Molnar said. "Except for one thing."

"What?" Xavier asked. All eyes went to Molnar.

Molnar pointed his thumb back to the perimeter wall. A patch of fence had been torn away from a gap in the wall, and a set of footprints marked the mud-splashed trail that a triceratops had paved on its way out of the valley. Xavier groaned and his head fell forward, clicking against the roll-bars of the jeep. He raised a finger in the air and did a circling motion for the jeeps to come together.

"Well," Xavier sighed. "Off to the real war."

SEASON OF THE WITCH

The front lines of the Vietnam War resembled particles sprinkled across a map, arbitrary representations of platoons marching from hill to hill on an ever-shifting chess board of unforgiving rainforests and impenetrable mountain landscapes. One such infantry platoon was straying dangerously close to an isolated jungle valley north of the DMZ, in search of a missing squad-mate that had marched off AWOL from the War in its entirety.

The platoon was part of C-Company, but they were far off course from their chartered destination. The Lieutenant of the squad was adamant that they capture the runaway soldier by any means necessary, regardless of the risks involved with traipsing through enemy territory. While the rest of their squad was investigating the trail left behind by their missing brother-in-arms, a trio of soldiers from the Third Squad of C-Company took a moment to assess their situation at the edge of a floodplain.

"Recon," an African American soldier sneered. "At least he's not sending us down any more tunnels. 'Member what happened to Stink? We'd be lucky to find half of that Buddha-boy if he hits one of those French mines. C'mon Doc, pass that over here. No hoggin'."

"Chill, Oscar."

Oscar, the African American soldier, was squatting with a pair of white soldiers at the edge of an elephant grass floodplain. One of the white soldiers, a wiry 18 year old with oily black hair dripping down to his ears, took a hit from a burning joint and passed it to Oscar. The black-haired white boy watched Oscar puff on the spliff, the cherry flashing with every hit.

[161]

"Good roll, Doc, good roll," Oscar said, nodding approvingly. His black-framed aviators bounced on the end of his stiletto-tip nose. Nobody in the squad had ever seen Oscar take the aviators off; not even on night patrols. There was always a cigarette on his lips after dark, to help light the way for the more frightened recruits of the squad.

"Keep it going," the greasy-haired white soldier said. "No stallin'."

Oscar tucked the joint between the extended fingers of the third soldier.

"Hit it 'n quit it, Frenchie," Oscar said, smacking the kid's helmet.

'Frenchie' Berlin almost dropped the joint as he flinched, but he kept his yellowing nails tight into the resin-stained paper. 'Frenchie' got his nickname for the ridiculous pencil-thin moustache that constantly outlined his upper lip. Frenchie's inability to grow anything other than a prepubescent boy's facial hair had resulted in relentless juvenile teasing and bullying throughout his two years of service in Vietnam. The inferiority complex that ensued propelled Frenchie to get tattoos from any dirty needle available in Saigon. Diluted-black calligraphy describing various recipes in foreign languages covered his exposed torso and arms.

"Me t'inks the gov'ment's up t'sometin'," Frenchie muttered through the joint. "Y'hearin' the radio reports back't base? Feathered lizards? Soldiers missing? Charlie Cong ain't got no'tin' t'do wit' it."

"Too much spooky shit in the grass," Doc said, plucking the half-smoked joint from Frenchie's clenched teeth. "Gotta smoke that pure stuff, none of that meth-opium shit Charlie's got."

"Golden rule," Oscar nodded. "Never smoke Charlie's stash."

[162]

"Heard," Frenchie grunted.

The three men nodded in silent agreement within their musky, herbal cloud. They had seen one of their squad-mates, poor 'Billy Boy' Peret, smoke a dead Viet Cong's pipe. The lethal dose of pure opium sent Billy Boy's 20-year-abstinent body into instant convulsions. He had cried with joy all through his seizures, foam bubbling from his mouth in gushing spouts of frothy-white bile.

"Gotta keep it clean," Doc said, exhaling a dense nimbus cloud.

It was the start of a new day; the sun was cooking the Vietnamese rainforest, brewing humidity as thick as clay beneath the multi-storied canopy. Rolling mist tumbled down from the forested foothills and sieved through the ocean of elephant grass. The soldiers' smoke was concealed completely within the mist. Despite the sun pouring its heat upon the clearing, the mist wouldn't clear out. Oscar couldn't shake the spooky feeling of Vietnamese eyes on the nape of his neck. He wiped the condensation from his aviators as the roach of the joint fell dead from his wet lips.

"We should get back," Oscar muttered. "'Fore old man comes looking for us, or else we get lost."

"Lost ain't so bad," Frenchie shrugged, leaning back into an earthen mound. "Shit, ground here's soft. May as well take a nap."

"Fuckin' fool," Oscar snapped. "Doc, Frenchie here thinks he's takin' a nap out here in Charlie country. Shit, just zip the dumb fuck in a body bag and leave 'im for Charlie. See they don't put a bayonet up his ass."

"I'm gettin' up," Frenchie said, pushing his hands against the lumpy mound. "Shit, my arms are sinkin' in here…"

[163]

"That's 'cause it *is* shit," Oscar snapped, slapping the helmet on Frenchie's head. "Get outta that 'fore you get an infection like Murphy."

"Rest in peace," Doc said, shaking his head.

"Lucky there ain't punjis in there," Oscar said. He grabbed Frenchie by the shoulders and pulled him free of the fecal mound. In his efforts to pull Frenchie out, Oscar tripped on a half-buried root and fell onto his back in the wet turf. He reached an arm back to grab his M16, prodding the dew-dappled earth with trembling fingertips.

"Lucky I ain't fall on my rifle, Frenchie," Oscar stammered. "You're real fuckin' lucky."

Oscar wrapped his hand around the plastic stock of his M16, but when he pulled, it refused to move. When Oscar looked over his shoulder, he saw a heavy boot pressing down on the trigger guard. In normal circumstances Oscar would have immediately panicked, but thanks to the THC, his coral-pink eyes merely skimmed over the tiger-striped uniform of the Special Forces soldier standing on his rifle.

"Don't panic," Molnar grinned. "I'm friendly."

"What in the fuck," Frenchie stammered, jerking to his feet while clumsily pointing his M60 at Molnar. "Where the fuck'd you come from? You SOS or somethin'?"

"He mean's 'SOF'," Doc said, raising his hands above his head.

"I know what I said," Frenchie spat over his shoulder.

"Don't panic," Oscar said from the marshy floor. "Keep cool."

[164]

Molnar side-stepped Frenchie's M60 and nudged the barrel aside. He rolled his shoulders, bringing the multi-lingual graffiti-scrawled Remington to his chest with a wry smile.

"Smells like somebody stepped in some shit," Molnar said. "Was it you, Frenchie?"

"How'd you know my name?" Frenchie barked, lowering the M60. "You been followin' us?"

"Charlie could hear you cats calling across the valley," Molnar said. "The rest of my squad's out in the grass. Rangling. You know how it is."

"Rangling Charlie?" Oscar said, sitting upright. He pushed the aviators back to his brow. "Sounds like SOF. Ain't any grunts talking like that 'less they're crazy."

"Like Stink," Doc grunted.

"Right," Oscar nodded. "Restin' 'n pieces."

"R-I-P."

"Smells like rituals are afoot," Molnar sneered. "Burning sage to cleanse the air for the spirits to breathe. Rest in peace, Stink."

"You ain't tellin' our Lt, are ya?" Frenchie asked. He took a step forward, bringing his sweating pink face inches from Molnar's hooked nose. "You ain't tryin' t'start nothin', right?"

"Every path starts somewhere," Molnar said, swinging the Remington over his shoulder. He withdrew a necklace from the depths of his tiger-striped fatigues and dangled it between Frenchie's bugging eyes. A small doe-skin pouch bounced on

[165]

the tip of Frenchie's nose from the leather strip. "We can start your path in the time it takes to smoke a pipe. How would you like that? Are you brave?"

"It ain't clean," Oscar said, shaking his head. "Don't smoke anything that sucker's got, Frenchie. We ain't 'bout to take your ass up them hills on a stretcher."

"Chopper'll lift him out in a bag," Doc said. "No sweat, no fuss, no muss."

Molnar was already untying the knot that bound the pouch shut.

"It'll only take ten, fifteen minutes," Molnar said. He knelt in the center of the three infantrymen and withdrew a ceramic pipe from the doe-skin pouch. It resembled a small paddle with a shallow recess for tobacco to be burned. The earthen brown pipe was adorned with finger-etched feathered serpents, Quetzalcoatl and crudely etched Aztec warriors with leopard-skins on their scalps. Molnar took an inch-long glass vial filled with red powder from the pouch and poured it into the pipe.

"That smack?" Oscar asked, peering over Molnar's shoulder.

"Opium?" Doc suggested, raising a finger in an astute manner.

"Jungle spice," Molnar said. He took a Zippo from his pocket and raised the ceramic pipe for all to see. "Extracted from *Psychotria viridis*. Quechua medicine-men call it *chacruna*. Take three puffs from the pipe, keep all the smoke in your lungs, and get ready for a ride to the other side."

"The wild side?" Frenchie asked.

"The wildest," Molnar winked. He extended the pipe. "You ready?"

Frenchie accepted the pipe in his cupped hands.

[166]

"It ain't clean," Oscar said, shaking his head. "Ain't never heard of nobody smokin' some Psycho-triage cha-cha-cru- cru shit."

Molnar placed the Zippo in Frenchie's clammy palm.

"Three hits," Molnar said, revealing his gleaming incisors. "No more."

"Frenchie-" Doc raised his hand, but it was too late.

Frenchie dropped to his ass beside Molnar in the mud and sucked three loads of flowery smoke into his lungs. The tattooed twenty-something was flopping and floundering against the mound of shit before the smoke could filter through his parted lips. Frenchie moaned enthusiastically as he flailed between Oscar and Doc, whom were both attempting to drag him from the dinosaur scat.

"The fuck'd you do to 'im," Oscar said, snapping his teeth at Molnar. "What the fuck'd you do to Frenchie?!"

"Blessed journey," Molnar said, crossing himself. "He'll return soon."

"*Molnar!*"

Molnar, Oscar, and Doc turned in unison as an interloper stumbled out from the elephant grass. It was Lalo Florez, the medic of Stalker Force. His bush-tanned face was wet with sweat and morning dew. Lalo lowered his M16 as he sprinted across the field to Frenchie's side.

"*Madre de dios,*" Lalo muttered. He flipped Frenchie onto his back and slapped his face gently. "What did you do to this kid, Molnar?"

"Enlightenment," Molnar smiled. "For the least likely to be enlightened."

[167]

"You know we aren't supposed to talk to grunts," Lalo said, looking back at Molnar. "We have to get these guys out of here before the you-know-what comes out from the grass. It's already following me."

"You got the bait?" Molnar asked.

"*Si*," Lalo said, opening his rucksack for Molnar to see. The soured-onion stink of the durian fruit struck the men before the bag was half-way open. Each thorny-green fruit was as big as a football and a delicacy for the runaway triceratops that Stalker Force had been tracking from the valley. Molnar and Lalo had been dispatched to help sweep the floodplain for the herbivore, but Molnar was prone to his momentary derelictions from duty.

"You're baiting Charlie with fruit?" Doc said, squinting.

"Sure," Lalo said, nodding. "Whatever Molnar said."

The elephant grass began to shift as a large animal ambled through. The bright-bloody crest of the triceratops sieved through the towering grass, the horn-tipped snout rising to sniff the sweet scent of burning Jungle Spice. Oscar and Doc both bounced back to their feet, backing away from the approaching herbivorous dinosaur. Lalo groaned irritably as he directed his attention from the quivering Frenchie to the inquisitive triceratops and back again.

"Hombre'll live, right?" Lalo asked, glancing at Molnar.

Molnar stood before the triceratops with his arms outstretched. The full-grown animal was nearly thirty feet long and as tall as an African Elephant. Molnar placed his hands around the beaked jaws of the triceratops as it chewed several pounds of root-bark.

[168]

"Get your hands off of that thing!" Lalo shouted.

"It'll be fine," Molnar said, stroking the triceratops's bulging cheeks. "Frenchie'll be fine, this trike'll be fine, we'll all be fine. Just gotta wait fifteen minutes for the rest of the team and for Frenchie to come home."

"*Frenchie?*" Lalo repeated.

"The fool flailing in your arms," Molnar said without looking back.

"*Stink*," Frenchie shouted, jumping upright. He nearly sent Lalo to the ground with the momentum of his resurrection. "Stink's alive! He's out there, Billy Boy too, they're out in space! I seen them up in the pyramids with all these aliens, angels, I don't even know, man, I—I—"

Frenchie couldn't tell if he had actually returned to his body from the void of psychedelic space. There was something like a dinosaur standing in front of him, except it was made of shifting geometric shapes all twisting and rotating into new positions before his eyes, but always maintaining the consistent shape of a dinosaur. It was like the 'three-horns' he had played with as a kid. The thing's eyes were like a pair of kaleidoscopic suns rotating and spinning over its parrot-beak jaws. It looked so real, he felt he could touch it.

"Come on," Molnar said, waving to Frenchie. "You know you want to."

"No, sit," Lalo implored, pinning Frenchie's shoulders against the mound of triceratops dung. To Molnar, Lalo hissed, "*What the fuck are you doing? You trying to get this chico killed?*"

Frenchie pushed Lalo aside and staggered over to the geometric miasma shaped like a triceratops. The closer he got, the more detailed the dinosaur's sapphire

[169]

scales gleamed, catching his eyes and filling his core with nostalgic warmth. Frenchie felt the nourishment of his inner child as he wrapped his poorly-tattooed arms around the snout of the triceratops.

The placid triceratops grunted apathetically, but otherwise ignored Frenchie's childish cooing. Molnar slapped the triceratops a few times between the pair of horns above its eyes and moseyed over to Lalo. The newest recruit of Stalker Force, a Cuban refugee that had seen the worst of Castro's regime, had suddenly been struck dumb in the face of a gentle dinosaur and a wildly hallucinating American kid from the front.

"Anybody wanna say why there's dinosaurs here?" Oscar said from behind a moss-draped log.

Doc poked his helmet up from behind the log.

"I would like some of that info as well, sirs."

"Classified," Molnar said with a jubilant shrug. "You know the drill."

"*There it is!*"

Xavier Wise and the rest of Stalker Force came pouring out from the tree-line. Xavier had his rifle aimed at the triceratops, but when he saw the three unfamiliar soldiers with Lalo and Molnar, he paused. Xavier squinted at the grown man sobbing against the confused triceratops's face. Andrei stepped beside him and grunted thoughtfully.

"Is that comrade, uh…"

"Petting a triceratops?" Xavier growled, enunciating forcefully through his teeth.

"No," Andrei said. "I was going to say 'crying', but yes. He appears to be petting a triceratops as well as crying. I can't help but feel a little confused by this development."

"Should we stop them?" Syd asked from behind Xavier.

The triceratops shook its head roughly, sending Frenchie's sandbag-silhouette sailing across the clearing. Xavier, Andrei, Syd and the snipers rotated their heads to follow each impact Frenchie's body made against the ground. Once the tumbling form of Frenchie finally slowed to a stop and lay flat, Lalo and Molnar sprinted across the clearing to check on him. The triceratops bellowed as it barreled downhill and away from the floodplain. Xavier sighed in solemn resignation.

"Fuckin' *Molnar*..."

THE ABYSS

The riverbank was fresh with recent rainfall, the foliage shimmering golden with the light of the sun hanging overhead, suspended like a lynched Apollo. The men of Stalker Force were lingering along the tepid stream, eyeing their reflections in the muddy wake. They had just captured and tethered their runaway triceratops, and a helicopter had air-lifted it back to the valley where it had originally migrated from. As the men waited for their own evac helicopter to arrive, they busied themselves with idle chat, passed cigarettes, and stories of splendor and misery.

Syd Kinane was there, but he was always in his thoughts, forever entangled with his own shaded past. He had originally been a member of Tiger Force, a specialized team made of the most violent and aggressive soldiers the US Military had deemed acceptable for service. It was an odd plan; take the most blood-soaked men from the front-line infantry and train them in the counter-guerilla tactics of the Green Beret. They were the barbarians of the Vietnam War, sent from village to village to extract the Viet Cong like maggots from a festering wound. There were no restrictions to their brutality; whatever it took to get their mission accomplished, they were granted every permission to do so.

As Syd rested on his haunches on the sandy riverbank, he played with a fern frond, plucking the soft tips between his calloused fingertips. His nails had grown to claws, worn down to fine points by the constant collaborations between his digits and the hefty, gnarled steel of his M60. The slightest touch of his skin seemed to make the fern frond in his hands wear away to a translucent, malleable pulp. It seemed to Syd as though his touch sieved the life from anything he grasped. Women, animals, the vegetation he clawed through during the war; they were rendered to decayed refuse upon interacting with Syd.

[172]

Syd tossed the frond aside and plucked another from the plume he was kneeling beside. As he worked the vegetation between his primeval hands, he thought of a book he had been forced to read in high school; Of Mice and Men. Syd's classmates had started calling him 'Lenny' after learning of the simple-minded character in the book. In a world of Georges, a Lenny was a beast of burden. As the friends he grew up with enjoyed themselves wrestling with cheerleaders and pothead vixens, Syd had been forced to wait on the porches of the high school parties, his only companion a pilfered bottle of whiskey and the moon watching him from its throne on high.

Poor Syd the Lenny; despite a love of poetry, his own craft wasn't seen as a worthwhile contribution to the art. Even with a scholarship he had only ever been seen as a brutish ape occupying the space where a scholar-to-be should sit. His professors saw worthlessness in his prose and detritus in the moral quandaries of his solipsism. He had been flunked for dubious reasons and cast to the dregs of L.A's skid row when his scholarship was finally terminated.

There was money to be had among the scabs and the scrubs. Somebody was always in desperate need of abuse; Syd the Lenny was left to collect scraps of cash among the teeth and clipped tips of tongues from the cement floors of basements where he had been paid to fight. Gangs desired Syd for his bulk and underground fighting circuits dreamt of paying him to throw a fight in their favor. Hurl southpaws at the beast; let David knock Goliath to his ass to the surprise of everybody in view. When Syd wasn't doling out concussions, he was receiving them for higher payouts and respect from the ringleaders of the fighting circuits.

The spectators would laugh and cheer when Syd the Lenny hit the ground. They would slap him across the face at the after-parties in seedy bars, beckoning him

[173]

to throw a fist, begging him to let them try their hand at toppling Goliath. Everybody wanted to be David, George, never the Lenny or the brute.

Syd would let them laugh.

When one of his fights ended in the death of a hulking Italian, the underground circuit tossed Syd to the wolves. The judge had made Syd's choices clear; find yourself in prison, awaiting the electric chair with a pack of cards and a nudie mag to waste away the time, or discover your truest self on the business end of an American rifle. There was promise of escape in Vietnam, where the poets and the Georges of the world were laid to waste by the great specter of war. Poor Syd the Lenny relented, accepting the possibility of death as a greater choice than a guaranteed demise with electrodes incinerating his scalp. He had lived life as a prisoner to his own hulking build; he refused to be a prisoner to any other establishment.

Other than the military, of course.

The fern frond in Syd's hand was rendered to a wet, green mash. He suddenly realized this and grunted in disgust, tossing the remains to the river. There was a ritual to the pattern, his habitual practice of feeding mangled life forms to the hungry current of Vietnam's primordial waters. Another village, another pile to feed to the ravenous Vietnamese rivers. When Syd reached for another leaf from the fern, he clearly saw another pile of bodies beneath his grasping fingers. As he gently plucked a frond, he felt the cold, bloated wrist of yet another dead villager in his grasp. As he began to pull apart the lush tips of the frond, his mind went to depths that frequently clawed forth from his dreams.

Napalm-soaked carcasses, the flesh stripping startlingly wet from moon-white bone within Syd's grasp. A heaving groan of disgust as he digs his fingers

[174]

between the fibia and ulna, getting a good hold, hefting the brittle frame into a pit amongst countless others. Breathing deep the sour fumes of stomachs splitting open when the bloated bodies strike the ground and spill their contents like Red Cross bags of rice for hungry villagers. Another handful of malleable flesh running wet, crimson and cold between his fingers, mosquitoes and flies biting at his eyes for a warmer offering of blood.

The parasites sang for their meals, buzzing against his ear drums, clawing deeper into the canals of his ears to make themselves heard. Dragging their skittering limbs against his skull, drumming his ear drums to the beat of his heart, hissing through the empty space of his cerebellum where sonnets were once spilled forth like the celestial tide of life that followed the Big Bang. The songs of the parasites shrieked through the abyss of his mind, reenacting the screams of desecrated villagers, the victims of his machete, his M60, his lead-weight fists and lacerating knuckles.

As a member of Tiger Force, Vietnam was Syd's for the taking. Every village brought the promise of a fresh bounty, drugs and women and children, whichever poison the men were inspired to seize. Syd would stroll through burning rows of thatch huts, his M60 resting over his shoulder, the screams of the raped and masticated crying forth from the shadows within straw shelters. There were trophies, of course; a finger sawed off from a man begging for god; an ear sliced neatly just beneath the scalp of a tribal elder; pliers clicking across teeth while tongues darted between parting lips.

The spoils of war.

Another frond was rendered to grease-paint between Syd's fingers, forgotten and dripping between his dancing fingers. He stared at the distance that

[175]

lied beyond Xavier Wise, Andrei Wynn, the men of Stalker Force and the jungle writhing through Vietnam, churning with exploding IED's and rippling anxiously with staccato firefights. Syd saw through the jungle, the distant mountain ranges, past the sky and into the depths of empty, ethereal space. Syd could see the black void where his mind returned to night after night, at first clutching himself in restless agitation upon the revelation of such a lifeless place before finally submitting to lying cold and naked like a stillborn fetus in his sleeping bag.

The screams no longer brought him to shivers; the songs of the dead and dying became as impotent as his dreams.

The poetry never returned to Syd's mind. His emotional outlets ran dry, blistering beneath the heat of an unforgiving sun that never set. He could see the shadows of his subconscious sitting deep within their cauldrons of filth, the mangled bodies of dead Vietnamese villagers writhing and copulating in the perpetual night inside his skull, begging and singing for his eventual return. A throne had been carved from the eddying slew of blood and bile as it ossified in the musty air, and it was promised as a final resting place for the creator of its den. Syd returned to his throne every night, sitting amongst the dancing dead that hurled shit and sluicing rotted flesh at his bare skin, laughing and jeering for him to finally close the madhouse, to end his life and end the memories that imprisoned the tortured souls of his victims.

As Syd dug his gnarled nails through his palm, stripping the flesh, a dim look of apathy was splayed across his face. The sun was fresh and hot on his gaunt cheeks, drying each bead of sweat to salt that stained his skin white like bleached bone. The pulse of the evac helicopter's rotor blades roared over the jungle canopy framing the river, and the black body of the craft slowly drifted down to meet the men of Stalker Force. As the rest of the team gathered their gear, the new medic Lalo

[176]

Florez looked down the length of the bank and noticed Syd clawing at his palms beneath the hovering sun. Lalo's eyes stretched wide with concern and he quickly jogged over.

"C'mon hombre, the helicopter's here," Lalo said. He snapped his fingers in front of Syd's face, but his apathetic mask didn't reveal any recognition.

Syd's eyes climbed from the abyss to meet Lalo's gaze, and a disinterested grunt crawled between his lips. He glanced down at his hands, saw the rosy sheen of fresh blood, and sloppily wiped the stains away on his pant legs. Syd climbed to his feet, clearing his throat.

"Good," Syd muttered. "Ready."

Lalo glanced over his shoulders at the rest of Stalker Force climbing inside of the helicopter, and he looked back at Syd warily. He wanted to rest his eyes on Syd's freshly bleeding hand but resisted the urge to do so, keeping his pupils pinned to Syd's face instead. He opened his mouth to speak, but the dead pits contained within Syd's irises made him falter and choke uncomfortably.

"You uh…you okay, hombre?"

"Yeah," Syd said, looking through Lalo to the abyss beyond. "Just day-dreamin'."

Syd dreamt of the abyss.

THE NIHIL RIVER GOD AND MAN

Sobek Colony was finally cornered.

Months of obsessive tracking, trial and error, and perseverance by Stalker Force had finally put a dent in the utahraptor population within the valley. The pockets of utahraptor families abandoned during the migration of the Cyclops Colony had been systematically destroyed by Stalker Force and Yutyrannus alike. Each utahraptor trail that Xavier followed seemed to lead only to starving, suffering dromaeosaurids that were easily put down. Other trails led to the utahraptor carcasses left behind in the wake of yutyrannus attacks.

The pair of yutyrannus that prowled through the valley rapidly painted their niche in the ecosystem with utahraptor blood. The fledgling cryolophosaurus families that remained began trailing after the yutyrannus, scavenging what they could from massacred utahraptors. After being outcompeted by the tyrannosaurs, kaprosuchus, quetzalcoatlus and deinonychus, the cryolophosaurus had been reduced to the status of oversized jackals.

By following the paths of the Yutyrannus, Stalker Force located what isolated utahraptor families remained and put them down. The men showed no remorse or mercy for the man-eaters; trophies were taken, claws and teeth were pried off with ka-bars, and feather pelts began to litter Stalker Force's war-room at Jericho's base. There was still the threat of the utahraptors that had originally fled, but the utmost concern remained the population within the valley. Until every utahraptor had been laid to rest, the research efforts of the CIA remained far too risky an endeavor.

The sole surviving utahraptors of Sobek Colony were isolated to nest site c, a small clearing located in the foothills of the south-western valley wall where the

[178]

jungle bled into the floodplains. At 0800, Jericho ordered Stalker Force to a small hill-top overlooking nest site c. The Hyenas, now under the orders of Mr. Crowley, remained within a huey-iroquois that was busy circling the tree-line surrounding the fields of elephant grass.

At 0900 the dawn sky resembled layers of soiled gauze, the purulent ulcer of the sun boring through bloody, coagulated cloud cover. The floodplains were silent, the ten-foot high elephant grass dappled with dew that worked prismatic magic with what sunlight sieved through the inflamed cloud cover. It seemed to Xavier Wise as if the flood-plains were actively anticipating the shells that were to inevitably render it to fire.

Xavier sighted nest site c through his binoculars. Sobek Colony, the last survivors of the valley's utahraptor population, was a paltry lot. Whereas Cyclops Colony had once possessed dozens of nests containing further dozens of young, this starving group consisted of only four nests with thread-bare egg clutches.

There was one female utahraptor per nest, with only a single beta male to protect the entire colony. Xavier didn't know where Sobek's hunting party was; he reasoned that they might have been slain by the yutyrannus, kaprosuchus, or even the Father T. rex. There was also a good possibility that they were still out on their late-night hunt, or they had starved to death during the weeks between their last sightings.

It was all the same to Xavier; Sobek was out of the way.

"What do you say, boss," Syd said. "Light 'em up?"

Xavier lowered the binoculars and turned to the rest of his team. Syd Kinane was squatting beside the radio, with exact coordinates of utahraptor nesting site c in-hand and ready for dispatch. Lalo and Andrei were kneeling on the grass, watching the fledgling colony of utahraptors from the edge of the hill-top. Molnar had a bottle of champagne pilfered from Jericho's office in his hands, both thumbs pressed against the cork.

"Not yet," Xavier said, scratching his chin. "Something's not right."

"This is it," Andrei said. "It's now or never."

"Let's flambé these birds," Molnar said, drumming his fingers along the champagne bottle. "It's only taken us, what, a year for this moment?"

"Bombers are on stand-by," Syd grunted.

"Something's not right," Xavier grumbled, returning the binoculars to his sunken eyes. "Look; Cryolophosaurus coming in from the east."

On the far left of the floodplain, Stalker Force could see the glimmering bodies of five cryolophosaurus slinking out from the tree-line. The last surviving matriarch led the way with a pair of beta males trotting on either side of her, grooming her ochre-dusted feathers and nipping at parasitic bugs. The nimble theropods were slowly making their way towards the nesting site, moving in a wide-arc around the colony. They could likely smell the scent of the dromaeosaurids in the air; the yutyrannus had to be near.

"There they are," Andrei said, pointing. "Coming in at 3 o'clock."

Xavier directed the binoculars north-west and saw the ghastly black-and-white speckled face of a yutyrannus rising above the elephant grass. The tyrannosaurid's iridescent emerald coat was near-seamless amongst the glistening blades of grass, but it was easy to follow the path they made. While the

[180]

cryolophosaurus were easy to spot, the yutyrannus appeared as a pair of spectral skulls floating through the elephant grass, trailed by slowly drawn lines of shadow.

"This might be your chance, Andrei," Xavier said. "Looks like we're about to finally see what the yutyrannus are capable of."

Andrei wove his fingers together beneath his chin.

"Don't doubt our quarry, comrade," he muttered. "That was our first mistake."

Sobek knew his colony's time had come.

It had been a year of hardships for the old alpha utahraptor; quarantines threatened the migration of the straggling survivors; over-saturation of predators throttled prey to intense scarcity. The constant pursuit of Stalker Force and the yutyrannus had put Sobek Colony into a state of extreme distress.

The female utahraptors were laying fewer eggs and the beta males were succumbing to starvation in favor of the hunting party and the breeders. Sobek was watching his colony from the periphery of the clearing. He was half-buried within a muddy pit, lying in wait as he listened to the approaching footfalls of the yutyrannus and cryolophosaurus. Sobek's heart began to beat more heavily as he felt the vibrations through his splayed forearms. He hissed softly and blew flecks of mud from his nostrils.

Sobek scratched at the grievous, deforming scar that spread across his throat and lower jaw. The kaprosuchus teeth embedded in his skull produced a mild ache; the arid dry-season air was causing the old wounds to enflame. Sobek wanted to pick

[181]

at the malformed scars with his fore-claws, but he didn't want to give away his position with any movement. The burrow he had made within the mud was covered with wiry rhododendron, and a single movement would ruin his cover.

Sobek noticed that the beta male utahraptor protecting the brood was visibly anxious, hopping to and fro like a panicked road-runner. The scent of cryolophosaurus was in the air; the acrid stench of rotten utahraptor carcasses picked clean.

The female utahraptors were beginning to ruffle their feathers in a show of agitation, flapping their forearms to send flurries of mud-droplets into the air. The eggs that had been laid in the nests were the only hope for the continuation of Sobek's colony; if their nesting site was compromised, there would be no hope of salvaging more than three eggs per surviving utahraptor.

Sobek understood the yutyrannus from his ritualistic failures.

The yutyrannus never attacked utahraptor nests head-on; they would lurk on the outskirts, circling the periphery as they surveyed their prey. Once the theropods removed any chance of protection for the females, they would slaughter the entire brood in one fell swoop and consume what remained. The Cryolophosaurus left nothing but bones and fragments of egg shells after the Yutyrannus completed the slaughter.

Sobek growled softly, burying his claws in the soil.

The wounds from his last encounter with the yutyrannus were still fresh.

The beta male protecting the female utahraptors began to squawk and shriek, trotting around the nesting site while fanning his forearm feathers. Sobek watched as the first yutyrannus, the male, sauntered through the elephant grass and
[182]

into the clearing. The male yutyrannus was always the first to move in for the kill; in order to protect his mate; he would face the full brunt of the utahraptors while she flanked the nest from behind.

The male yutyrannus was directly across the nest site from Sobek, but the tyrannosaurid couldn't see him. The male yutyrannus, distinguishable from his mate by his brighter red nasal crest and longer brow horns, rumbled lowly as he paced around the beta male utahraptor.

The male yutyrannus was a few feet taller, several feet longer, and nearly a metric ton heavier with muscle. The beta male utahraptor could do little more than feign from left to right as the larger predator approached.

Sobek watched from his burrow as the beta male spread its forearms, waving the feathers that draped its limbs like the ornamental robes of an ancient warrior. Sobek remained hidden from the yutyrannus, tucked out of sight beneath the clustered rhododendron that choked the tree-line of the clearing.

Sobek glanced to his left, where another member of his hunting party was half-buried in the mud. The submerged utahraptor glanced at Sobek and blew the grime from its nostrils with a hearty snort. Sobek bared his teeth, signifying a clear message to the other male for silence.

A heavy foot crunched down through the rhododendron to the right of Sobek. Careful not to get his crown of tusks ensnared in the wiry branches, Sobek slowly rotated his head to watch as the female yutyrannus waded past. The female yutyrannus was still several hundred pounds heavier than Sobek, but she possessed a clear weakness; the naivety of trusting her mate.

[183]

Sobek watched as the female yutyrannus strode fully into the clearing, spreading her stout forelimbs, howling to her mate across the nesting site. The female utahraptors pivoted in their nests, chattering and yowling in panic. The beta male utahraptor turned to accost the new threat.

The male yutyrannus's jaws snapped around the back of the beta male's neck, wrenching the smaller theropod off of its feet and throwing it aside. The beta male tumbled, the wounds in his neck spurting arterial blood across the soggy marsh floor.

This was it; now or never.

As silent as the mist of Vietnam's breath, Sobek leapt from his burrow and pounced onto the arched back of the female Yutyrannus. Another member of Sobek's hunting party leapt from a muddy tunnel and latched onto the left flank of the female yutyrannus. The yutyrannus bellowed as she struggled beneath the weight of the two utahraptors, buckling to her knees into the muddy basin.

Sobek kicked furiously at the calves of the female Yutyrannus, lacerating the taught leather flesh and revealing the glistening white of her bones. The female writhed as she sank into the softened soil, submerging deeper the more she tried to fight against the weight of the utahraptors.

The second hunting party utahraptor clamped his jaws around the female yutyrannus's forearm and raked his claws through her shoulder socket. The female yutyrannus yowled in pain as her arm was ripped away in the jaws of the utahraptor and thrown across the field, where it splashed heavily into a leech-ridden puddle.

The male yutyrannus paused his assault on the beta male utahraptor upon hearing the screams of his mate. The devil-horned predator's lips pulled back as he

[184]

snarled vehemently through four-inch fangs. The male yutyrannus howled and charged, his wide-splayed feet pounding through the meter-deep mud. The beta male utahraptor scrambled to get in the way of the male yutyrannus and the female utahraptors, but the demon's eyes were set solely on Sobek.

Sobek roared, and the hunting party echoed his screams of bloodlust.

A second pair of hunting party utahraptors pounced from their muddy burrows and struck the male yutyrannus from either side. The male yutyrannus stumbled, but quickly pivoted on his heel and swung his tail against the side of a utahraptor's head, snapping its lower jaw in half.

The broken-jawed utahraptor screeched as it hit the ground, but its screams were silenced by a well-placed kick to the throat from the yutyrannus. The utahraptor's throat was immediately flayed open, dripping wet and raw.

Sobek hissed in frustration as he wrestled atop the female yutyrannus. She was hemorrhaging from her exposed shoulder socket, but it wasn't enough to quell the fight in her. The female yutyrannus twisted around, kicking one leg free from the mud, and rolled onto her back, smothering Sobek beneath her.

Sobek felt his ribcage folding inward from the weight of the female yutyrannus. He heard the snap of his own bones breaking, felt the yutyrannus's hot blood trickling down the ravines of his scarred throat. Using his claws the way he had observed the therizinosaurus, Sobek burrowed through the mud and slipped out from underneath the half-submerged female yutyrannus.

The body of Sobek's hunting partner was splayed atop the female yutyrannus. The female yutyrannus had bitten through the utahraptor's neck with a snap of her jaws, and his stump of a neck was gushing burgundy blood over her

[185]

iridescent coat. The female yutyrannus had one leg completely buried in the mud, and her remaining arm was mired down to the elbow.

Sobek kicked the female yutyrannus just below the sternum, sinking his killing toe-claw down to the base of her gut. The female yutyrannus yowled, kicking furiously, but it was too late to stop Sobek's methodical attack.

Sobek jerked his leg back, vivisecting the female yutyrannus in one fluid slice as expertly as a field surgeon. Organs of every shade and shape slipped forth from the laceration and splashed into the mud around the dying yutyrannus. Sobek immediately redirected his attention to the male yutyrannus bellowing across the clearing.

The male yutyrannus was running around the shrieking female utahraptors with the last member of Sobek's hunting party hanging from his right flank. The male utahraptor attempted to climb up the side of the yutyrannus, but its talons kept slipping through the yutyrannus's thick proto-feather coat. The yutyrannus swung his shoulders aggressively and the utahraptor fell to the ground.

The yutyrannus lunged for the utahraptor's throat, but a well-timed kick split the titan's jowls open into a hideous Cheshire grin.

Sobek screamed at the male yutyrannus, distracting it long enough for the other utahraptor to slip away. Sobek charged across the clearing, lowering his body as he ran. He tightened his leg muscles and sprang through the air, sailing over the heads of the nesting female utahraptors. The yutyrannus only caught a glimpse of airborne greenery blurring towards him before Sobek collided with his neck.

The yutyrannus was knocked off of its feet, and when it struck the ground the air was punctured by the *crack* of a fractured femur. The clearing suddenly went

[186]

still, the female utahraptors silencing their screams, the beta male no longer writhing and yowling in pain. The floodplain held its breath as the lone surviving yutyrannus barked and chortled in pain, its maned throat constricting with the force of its blood-curdling braying.

Sobek climbed on top of the male yutyrannus, planted a foot over the theropod's eye socket, and brought down his scythe-blade toe talon. The yutyrannus's yowls of pain climbed to deafening decibels, and with a twist of the claw, the apex predator was silenced. Sobek stood tall, arched his neck back, and screamed victoriously to the infectious morning sun.

It was the start of a new day; another chance for Sobek's colony.

"*Jesus*," Xavier exhaled.

Molnar popped the champagne bottle, spraying an arc of crystalline foam high into the air. Andrei grumbled and got out of the way of the shower. Lalo wrestled with Molnar for the first pull from the high-necked bottle. Syd put his back to the conflict and started to urgently feed the coordinates of nest site c into the radio.

Xavier felt flies buzzing in and out of his gaping mouth as he watched Sobek, the scarred utahraptor, the infamous alpha with a crown of kaprosuchus tusks. He could scarcely believe what he had just seen. He remembered the chance encounter with Sobek amongst the therizinosaurus, the look in Sobek's eyes as the theropod observed the gargantuan herbivores emerging from the cover of the earth.

"When those utahraptors sprang the trap," Andrei said, getting close to Xavier's ear. "Did it remind you of anything?"

[187]

"Yeah," Xavier exhaled shakily. "The Viet Cong."

"What?" Andrei exclaimed, shouting over the roar of incoming jets. "No, the therizinosaurus! That alpha, Sobek, he must have learned from watching them. I've never seen anything like it; I mean, we've seen all of the evidence for the intelligence of the utahraptors, the misdirection, but implementing what they've observed other species doing and applying it to their own defense? It's astounding!"

"It's horrifying," Xavier muttered. "They should all be destroyed."

"I've heard that before," Andrei said, wagging a finger. "But I'm starting to think it's all for naught. This is just the last of the population in the valley; we still have to take care of the utahraptor colony that already escaped, and all of the rogue families that fled during the construction of the perimeter. I'm afraid these animals may prove to be a greater threat than we could have ever imagined."

"Charlie fuckers," Molnar laughed. "I almost respect them, y'know."

"Respect the dead," Syd said. "Fuck the living."

The droning engines in the sky reached a climax, and the black body of a bomber jet swept over the hill-top, casting its shadow onto the floodplains below. Sobek and the surviving utahraptors screamed in defiance as the bombs fell upon the floodplains, incinerating the fields of elephant grass with blossoming napalm.

Xavier and the rest of Stalker Force watched in silent awe as the endless sea of elephant grass was consumed by towering pillars of flame, and the final screams of Sobek and the utahraptors were finally swallowed within the breathless roar of Jericho's righteous hell-fire. The caterwauling of the infernal utahraptors made Xavier think of the Viet Cong he had slaughtered throughout the course of the

[188]

Vietnam War, and he swore he could see the ghosts of the dead Vietnamese rising like smoke from the fire.

Utahraptors or Viet Cong; the screams were all the same to Xavier Wise.

EPILOGUE – THE PANTHER

Vietnamese men had infiltrated Stalker Force's valley.

Lockheed YO-3 'Quiet Star' reconnaissance planes descended upon the
Valley at the behest of General Jericho. The light-weight propeller-driven Quiet
Stars skimmed the perimeter walls to watch out for any dinosaurs attempting to
breach the quarantine. On a relatively tepid day, one such Quiet Star detected a
human settlement situated within the north-west quadrant of the valley, near the
abandoned Russian compound. The pilot of the Quiet Star had noticed the ragged
tents of repurposed burlap rice sacks and notified General Jericho immediately to the
presence of potential Viet Cong.

It was a mystery to Jericho how such a paltry group could have managed to
infiltrate the valley. He ordered Mr. Crowley and the Hyenas to investigate the
potential Viet Cong encampment. There had been a small Viet Cong presence in the
valley when it had been under Russian control, but upon seizing the territory the
American forces had seldom encountered any Vietnamese.

Most of the NVA and Viet Cong had spread rumors of the Russians'
experimentation in the remote wilderness. Tall tales of feathered dragons and
rapacious demons had begun to spring forth from every communist outpost within a
hundred mile radius of the valley.

Nguyen watched the Russian compound, the 'ash-tray', rotating below as
the Hyenas' helicopter orbited the barren clearing. Mr. Crowley was sitting across
from Nguyen with their two new squad-mates flanking him. The Hyenas were
wearing their standard black fatigues and woolen balaclavas. Nguyen had gone on
several missions with his new team-mates, 'Horus' and 'Aiwass', but had spoken
little with either of them. The most he could gauge of their identities was that Horus

[190]

was of middle-eastern descent and that Aiwass was an African American. Otherwise, they were blank slates; doppelganger pawns for Jericho.

Stalker Force had ridden along as back-up in case the situation was escalated by the prehistoric wildlife. Xavier and Andrei were the only ones currently awake; the rest of Stalker Force were passed-out from their week-long excursion cornering and destroying Sobek Colony's final nesting site. Stalker Force had been instructed to remain within the helicopter a safe distance away until an evac was ordered; emergency or otherwise.

The helicopter quickly settled down on the opposite end of the abandoned compound from the ramshackle campsite. The Hyenas hopped out of the aircraft, weapons in hand, and the helicopter lifted off before any potential incoming rounds could strike its steel carapace. Nguyen kept his M16 to his cheek as he followed Mr. Crowley and the others to the burlap tents.

A pair of water buffalo were tethered to a twenty-foot banana tree beside the moth-chewed tents. Nguyen didn't think the soft green trunk of the tree would stand a chance restraining the live-stock if they were scared off by a dinosaur. If the people that had built the camp were still alive, they clearly didn't know what kind of danger their beasts of burden currently faced.

One of the buffalo began to bray, stamping its feet. Mr. Crowley narrowed his eyes at the velveteen black bovine. He glanced at Horus and flicked his wrist towards the buffalo. Horus ran past Nguyen and Mr. Crowley, unsheathing his machete.

Nguyen looked away; he heard the blade swiping through the herbivore's throat, the waves of blood spilling by the bucket-load. When he looked back, the dim-witted beast was down to its knees, struggling to remain aloft. Horus gave the

[191]

animal a rough kick and it rolled to its side, no longer moving. The other buffalo was watching the men with warm, wet eyes. Horus slit its throat before it could become a distraction.

With the animals slain, the Hyenas were able to scour the camp-site more freely. Horus and Aiwass stood with their rifles at the ready as Nguyen and Mr. Crowley dug through the tents. There were paltry cooking pots, small rations of rice, and fruit picked from durian and fig trees. Nguyen found himself reflecting as he handled journals written in Vietnamese, letters dictated to friends and family, photographs that mirrored the brothers he had lost long ago to the war.

It had been years since Nguyen had last seen his family. His older brothers had lost their lives to the Viet Cong after being drafted into the South Vietnamese Army. NVA bombings had destroyed their village, and his parents burned to death within their immolated hut. Nguyen felt tears coming to his eyes as he stared into a yellowing family portrait that he had plucked from a tattered cloth bag.

He had lost so much, yet gained nothing.

Vietnam was no longer a priority for Jericho. Stalker Force was being redirected to the neighboring countries of Laos and Cambodia, and with it, Nguyen and the Hyenas would resume their clandestine work in the shadows. All that mattered to Jericho was the balance of power between the United States and the Soviets. Everything that had once constituted Nguyen's life; his native homeland, the Vietnamese people, his heritage; had become irrelevant to Jericho.

Nguyen curled his fist around the photograph as tears tapped the creased paper. He thought of Scarecrow, Jericho's bastard of a replacement for Bishop, the look in his eyes as Nguyen delivered thoughtless blows with his machete. Caustic acid roiled within his core.

[192]

There was nothing left for Nguyen; no home to return to, no life to resume beyond the construct of institutional violence. All that remained of Nguyen's existence was the need to continue propagating the violence that had removed so much worth from his world. There was money to be made killing for Jericho; possibly enough for him to build a new life once the world had abandoned its petulant lust for war.

"*Dừng lại!*"

Nguyen raised his head; Mr. Crowley was shouting outside. He heard Mr. Crowley repeat the phrase, '*Stop*,' in Vietnamese. Nguyen shoved the family portrait into his pocket without thinking, then grabbed his M16 and ducked through the burlap sheet. Mr. Crowley, Aiwass, and Horus were standing outside, aiming their rifles across the clearing.

Nguyen turned just as Mr. Crowley began firing his M16. Nguyen flinched, shocked by the sudden crackling of automatic fire. He saw their quarry across the clearing; young Vietnamese men collapsed at the edge of the compound as bullets perforated their starving frames. Aiwass and Horus began firing as well, chasing the falling bodies to the ground with lines of lead.

It was over before Nguyen could even process what was happening.

"Looks like…five VC killed, no shots fired," Mr. Crowley said, scratching the bridge of his nose. "Panther, collect the dead and bury 'em."

"No-no shots fired?" Nguyen stammered. "But you killed them?"

"Collect the dead," Mr. Crowley said. "Or better yet, leave 'em. No sense bothering with the bodies when they'll end up inside of some dinosaurs in an hour."

[193]

"Were they armed?" Nguyen asked, looking at Horus.

Horus shrugged, turned around, and walked across the clearing to the bodies. Nguyen watched as Horus glanced over the twitching, bleeding carcasses. Horus took a few grenades from his belt and dropped one onto each of the dead Vietnamese.

"They were armed," Horus called back. "Grenades, probably salvaged or stolen from dead American infantry."

Mr. Crowley took the radio from Aiwass's rucksack and repeated Horus's statement into the headset. Mr. Crowley then requested an evac, stating the area was 'secure from Viet Cong presence' and safe for landing. Nguyen stared at his captain, his jaws grinding audibly. Horus came back from the slain victims and started burning the personal effects of the campsite.

Nguyen dragged his boots all the way up to the dead Vietnamese. A cold numbness swam through his extremities as he searched the bodies for any proof that they had been Viet Cong. The dread that came with searching through the belongings of the dead had a way of emptying Nguyen's body of any emotion other than anxiety. When he discovered that they were all unarmed, the chasm within Nguyen's core began to fill with wretched heat.

Righteous fire burned through Nguyen's heart.

"Panther, get back here," Aiwass shouted. "Evac's coming."

"Leave 'im," Nguyen heard Mr. Crowley grunt. "He's probably making sure they weren't any of his own. Undercover Charlie. Only reason he's here is 'cause Jericho won't let me nix his ass."

[194]

"Half-fried panko," Horus laughed.

Automatic rifle-fire screamed throughout the clearing. Mr. Crowley dropped to a prone position as live ammunition popped and whistled over his head. Horus was struck twice in the chest; shards of bone protruded from his sternum as he fell back beside Mr. Crowley.

Aiwass attempted to return fire, but a runaway bullet cleaved through the space between his eyes. Grey matter splashed from the exit-wound across the banana tree and Aiwass fell spasming into the blood of the slaughtered buffalo.

The fire-fight was over in seconds.

Mr. Crowley raised his head from the half-dried mud and a boot connected with the bridge of his nose. He screamed in pain, dropping his rifle to cover his face. Another swinging boot caught him in the jaw, twisting his head around and rolling him onto his back. A slender young Vietnamese man dropped on top of Mr. Crowley and started strangling him, fingers tightening around the base of his neck.

"Fucking *Charlie*," Mr. Crowley choked. "*Fish-eyed gook!*"

Nguyen panted through his teeth as he slammed Mr. Crowley's head against the ground. He took a hand off of Mr. Crowley's neck to reach for the machete sheathed to his belt. A fist thrown by Mr. Crowley collided with Nguyen's temple, jarring him. Nguyen had one hand around Mr. Crowley's throat, his knees pinning Mr. Crowley's elbows to the ground, one hand feeling for the hilt of his blade…

Mr. Crowley slammed the palms of his hands against Nguyen's ears, stunning him. Nguyen briefly relinquished his grip on Mr. Crowley's throat. Mr.

[195]

Crowley ducked into Nguyen's chest, hooked his arms underneath Nguyen's arm pits, and tackled him forward.

Nguyen fell onto his back with Mr. Crowley on top. There was the flash of sunlight reflecting off of steel, and Nguyen saw Mr. Crowley's machete swinging down. Nguyen twisted to the side as the machete chopped into the ground beside his head, nicking the tip of his ear. Nguyen shrieked and swung his elbow back, cracking Mr. Crowley's lower jaw loose.

Nguyen scrambled away from Mr. Crowley, panting and unthinking, acting purely from primal instinct. He could hear Mr. Crowley struggling to get upright, withdrawing the machete from the dirt behind him. Nguyen dove to his M16, grabbed the rifle with both hands, and rolled swiftly to his feet.

Silence.

Nguyen quickly turned, aiming his rifle back to where Mr. Crowley had been. A mass of ferns and palm fronds churned through the mud, Mr. Crowley's exposed arms flailing out from beneath. The shaggy neck of a utahraptor withdrew from the mud. The utahraptor's tawny eyes skimmed over Nguyen's slack-jawed face.

Mr. Crowley's innards hung from the utahraptor's jaws.

Nguyen aimed his rifle at the utahraptor, taking plaintive steps back from the carnivore. The dromaeosaurid didn't take its eyes off of Nguyen; it cocked its head inquisitively, huffing deeply through its nostrils. Nguyen turned to run, but saw three more utahraptors on the opposite end of the compound, collecting the dead Vietnamese in their feather-laden forearms.

The scavengers ignored Nguyen.
[196]

The powerful pumping of rotor blades echoed from the sky. The utahraptors rose from their claims, grunting and cawing to one another as the helicopter returned to the compound. Nguyen watched as the utahraptors carried the dead back to the jungle, away from the helicopter before they could be seen.

Nguyen remained where he stood, bloodied and bruised, but alive. The utahraptors had spared him; when the helicopter picked him up, Xavier took note of the feathers littering the clearing. As the aircraft flew south to Jericho's base, Xavier studied Nguyen cautiously.

"So what happened back there?" Xavier asked.

Nguyen thought of the slaughtered Vietnamese, the feeling of the M16 bucking into his shoulder as he had fired upon Horus and Aiwass. He tasted blood; some of it had been Mr. Crowley's falling upon his face. Nguyen savored the horrible strength building in his core, the gratification of righting an almighty wrong upon his people.

"Five VC dead," Nguyen muttered. His vacant eyes penetrated Xavier's mud-rimmed pupils. "Utahraptors killed the rest of the team. I don't know why I'm alive."

"Maybe for something greater," Xavier shrugged, looking out the window. "That's all we can hope for. To be destined for something better than Vietnam."

"And you?" Nguyen asked, tilting his head back. "What about Stalker Force?"

"For us, the hunt has just begun," Xavier said. "We're flying out to Cambodia tomorrow. Kaprosuchus have been appearing in the rivers. Utahraptors have been seen as far as China. Deinonychus and stygimoloch are all over south-east Asia. We've also received word of quetzalcoatlus in Malaysia and Indonesia."

"The migration has begun," Andrei said.

"And so has the hunt," Xavier nodded.

Nguyen felt his lips curl into an involuntary smile.

"So it has."

Acknowledgements

First and foremost I would like to thank my family and friends for supporting me with their love throughout the process of my writing career. I wouldn't have had the motivation or passion to pursue this craft if it weren't for their motivation. A few folks in particular I'd like to thank include Jason Wise, Lewis Connell, Brian Flores, Andy Huynh, James Lancaster, Sean Markey, Greg Noneman, Jack De La Mare, Tom Parker, Mark Lim, Jeremy Moore, and Bill 'Liam' Hall.

This book wouldn't have been possible without the support of the Primitive War fan community. For anybody interested in joining in on the discussion, look up the Primitive War Discussion group on facebook. There you'll find the most recent artwork, updates, interviews, and news on everything related to Primitive War. In addition, I would like to refer readers to check out Prehistory – A Traveler's Guide podcast, The Bastard Sermon Podcast, Jurassic Outpost, and Sean The Dino Guy's articles on Geek Ireland.

Last but not least, a million debts are owed to the Primitive War Creative Team. These are the artists currently involved in the project, as well as their contributions. Check out their work on their deviant art, artstation, and facebook accounts. You can also find all of their contributions to Primitive War in the Primitive War Discussion group and on our facebook page. The cover artwork for this novel was done by Raph Lomotan and the text was added by Neil Kaskoun.

Bruno Hernandez – Bestiary illustrations

Raph Lomotan – Concept artwork

Babisu Kourtis – Comic illustrations

Neil Kaskoun – Concept artwork

Wyn Lacabra – Concept artwork

Justin Trevor Comley – Cover artwork

Allan Palmer – 3D models

Much love and many blessings. Thanks for reading!

-Ethan Pettus

Printed in Great Britain
by Amazon

20271142R00116